Like Water

MJ WHYMAN

Lavender Button Books

To my friend, Tina

Who always believed this was possible

***

He's washed the blood from his hands. Proper scrubbed them, all the way up to the elbows like you see doctors doing, but he keeps finding scraps under his nails and in the creases of his palms. It stinks. He's washed and washed and still he can smell it – that cold metallic smell that catches the back of the throat and excites and sickens all at once. He should feel sickened - but he doesn't. Dully, he wonders if this is the way it will always be.

He's alone in the dark. The city hums outside his window and far away there is a sound of sirens. He sits waiting for the moment, for something to happen.

Across the hall, he can hear her whispering, even though it is long gone midnight. Her voice jolts. She giggles, a crackling, unnatural sound as she pantomimes out a show of love. His mother.

He wonders for a moment at the word: `mother'. Somewhere he thinks he should feel warmth and softness at the word, but she has never been warm and soft – not to him.

She tells him to call her `Aggie' so that her varied and various `gentlemen callers' (her words) will think he's her lodger and not her kid. Sometimes he calls her `mum' just to piss her off and then the men look at her sharply and she laughs her plastic-shredding laugh and pulls them closer. The brittle, snake-sharp eyes spit at him across their shoulders.

Not that he cares. Not anymore. He's not the little kid he once was; the kid who climbed into the bottom of her bed in the early hours of the morning just to be near someone; who would break glasses just for a touch, even if it was a slap.

That was long ago and he feels a strange separation from her now, as if she is someone he heard about once. Some sad, fading woman who smiles and simpers and plays at love for some sense of belonging. Of worth.

Mother.

Alone in the dark, he wonders if she ever loved him. Carrying around a large lump of love for nine months certainly hadn't helped her mood – if there was any love in the conception.

Once upon a time, when he was very little and she was mellow on wine, she told him she had loved his father and he had wanted to believe it. But now he thought that she probably made it up. Like the name, his name. A name no-one else had. Ironic really, that it was a good name.

Mercutio. He was six when he asked why his name was different and she told him the story of the Montagues and Capulets, lingering on the death of the hot-headed, misinformed friend.

"A curse on both your houses," she said, "<u>both</u> your houses…"

The acid in her eyes stripped away his skin and bored little holes in his skull: a curse; a curse; a curse…

But he knew it was a good name. Mercutio, like Mercury, the metal that's not a metal, that can flow like water and change and poison. A good name.

It was one good thing his mother managed. She
managed another good thing too: because of her, he
met him.

ONCE

<u>Mercutio</u>

She slams the door behind me, cutting off the bad words that are falling out of her mouth like bullets and I don't look back. I scramble away, away, up the stairs, up and up until she won't be able to find me anymore.

At the very top, the big windows look out over London – grey buildings in the grey day. There is rain on the glass, like speckles. I just stand and look at the city so far away from me – like I'm a pilot in a plane, or an alien who can't find a place to land. I want to spread out my arms and pretend to fly, but I'm afraid someone will laugh.

("What a pillock," she says, "I swear there's something wrong with you.")

Somewhere someone opens a door and I stand very still. I don't want her to find me. Not yet. She's still too cross. I dunno what I did. Ate too much maybe or watched too much telly or just made her remember that I live where she does. It comes out of nowhere: I'm just sitting there and next thing, she slaps me or grabs me by the arm or the hair. I don't know why. She says it's because I'm an ungrateful little shit. I keep trying to be grateful, but I don't know what I'm supposed to do.

After a while I start to get cold. It is November and the cold of the tiles melts up into my toes and then my bones. I forgot my coat. Aggie was too fast.

I decide that it might be better to go back down – be on the stairs closer to home for when she opens the door.

Maybe her friend will see me and then she will have to let me in.

When Bettina finds me, I am curled up like a hedgehog on the steps at the corner of the stairwell. Aggie still hasn't opened the door, so I am curled tight, with my T-shirt stretching over my knees and my head down. When I see the brown boots stop in front of me, I don't want to look up. I am ashamed that she is looking at me: a scraggy, dirty kid, in scraggy, dirty clothes on the stairwell of a scraggy, dirty tower block where the concrete stairs are hard and cold.

I have been here for a while. I don't have a watch, but the cold has bitten into me. I can feel it reaching from the concrete into my bones and from my bones, into my heart. A wind is curling its invisible fingers up the stairs and up my nose. It smells of snow. All I can do is wait. Wait for Aggie to remember that its November and cold and I am eight.

("You're not a little kid anymore – just grow up!")

I am eight and this is the world: concrete, cold and waiting for Aggie to let me in. I just wait. There is nothing else to do.

Until Bettina is here. She is like a radiator. The warmth of her mists up the window and her hands are like toast on my shoulders. When I look up, her teeth flash all white behind full, lip-sticked lips. She smells of cinnamon.

"Where you live, baby?" she asks, taking my hands in her warm ones and rubbing them so that they turn red over the knuckles. I have never been called `baby' before and I don't know what to say. All I can do is look at her. She is wearing a green and gold head wrap and her skin is warm brown like a conker. She shines.

I want to say something about being locked out – about a mistake, but I can't find the words to explain, so I just sit quiet and let her rub my hands.

"Why's your hair so white?" says the little kid behind her.

Like that, I love him. He doesn't see that my clothes are stained and thin, or that my cheek is bruised or that I am ugly and skinny. He doesn't see the outside, he just sees me.

"It's not white, stupid, it's blonde," I say.

His mother tuts and smiles.

"Heee," she sighs in a long, laughter-sparkled breath, "come, chile."

 She takes me home without a second thought, just leads me – her soft hand warm against my skin like a blanket. And I just go. It's cold on the stairs and she is warm.

 Her flat is same as ours, but it is bright and warm like a nest. Even though I say I'm okay, she makes me have a bath and get warm. She even puts bubbles in. I want to say I don't need them, I'm not a little kid, but I've never had bubbles before.

When I bath, she lets me close the door and stay as long as I want, but I get afraid she'll be cross, so I don't stay too long.

She finds me some clothes from her boy. They are a bit too short and a bit too loose, but they smell like – like clean is supposed to smell – like morning. And then she feeds me Birdseye custard with stewed, spiced apples.

Just like that, suddenly God sees me and suddenly He shows me that people can live this way – where the world is full of colour and spice.

I feel important, here in this flat with Bettina's bowl of stewed apples in my hands and her voice running like ripples of warm milk. As if I matter. I don't know how it happens, but like you get warm in the sun, suddenly they matter to me too. Just like that.

More than matter. They fill me up.

" An' this is my boy, Romeo," she gives him a little squeeze that makes him smile, "like the Beckham's boy, you know."

"And Shakespeare's boy," I try, because I know that.

But she laughs and shakes her head: "I dunno about that, darlin'."

She is all warmth and bustle, like I imagine Winnie the Pooh's mum must be. She is the most beautiful woman I have ever seen with her eyes always wrinkling in a smile.

Someday soon, I will learn that she is fiercely independent. Abandoning the `rubbish man' who married her and making her own way, determined that Romeo will be better.

When I know her well, she will tell me that she is the daughter of an immigrant and one of seven children who lived crowded together in a small council house.

"My dad worked his backside off," she will say. "But all that fightin' the system made him old before his time.."

They live up-country, her family. She followed the useless man to London and now is here to stay. She shrugs and smiles: 'Life is what you make it.'

It's just her and Romeo. Like me and Aggie. But not. Bettina is warm and soft and loves her boy. She is everything I think a mum should be.

I don't want to ever leave. I snuggle into the warmth and the hot chocolate, listening to Romeo's cheerful chatter when we play snakes and ladders. It feels like a miracle. Like I'm suddenly in a different world.

I don't want to go back home where everything feels cold.

 My stomach sinks when I hear a door slam and Aggie's voice like paint stripper against the grey stairwell. I don't know why she wants me back – perhaps she is worried about being reported. I try to ignore her, but Bettina's face frowns as she listens.

"That your mama, baby?" she asks, the word 'mama' sounds weird in her velvety warm tones. I want to say 'no'; that 'mama' is the furthest word away from Aggie that anyone can imagine, but there is a miserable small shame in me and all I can do is nod.

"Oh, baby, she will be worried!"

She puts my dirty clothes in a carrier bag, as if sending them home will clean them and bundles me to the door.

"Hello?" she calls, "Mercutio's mum! I have him 'ere..."

Aggie's face appears around the corner of the stairs, her mouth smiling a smile that doesn't reach her eyes. I know she is taking in Bettina and her bright clothes; me and my borrowed ones.

"There he is! I didn't know where he'd got to, the scamp," she waves me to her impatiently. "I hope he didn't bother you."

"No, no, not at all," Bettina's hand slides off my shoulder as I walk away. "Come back to play with Romeo any time, darlin'. You go safe, now."

My mother reclaims me, all brittle play-acting and fake high-pitched concern. When I follow her downstairs, I turn to see Romeo watching me. His dark eyes x-ray into my heart.

What can I do – I am a little kid and she is my mother. Now.

But I have new possibilities and suddenly there is no going back to where I was. I want to shout and jump, but I stay quiet.

I don't get dinner because I have been "a little shit, going off and begging from those people," but Bettina's apples and custard are a warm secret in my belly when I curl under the thin duvet and slip into a sleep that feels like a promise.

Romeo

I don' know where he came from. I am just walking up the stairs, counting and thinking of the apples Mum made for lunch and then there he is. Like magic.

I haven't never seen him before. Not here and not at school. I think I would remember, even though Mum says my head is in the clouds. I think I would know him, that boy just sitting on the stairs like he ain't got no home.

I ain't never seen no-one like him. I wonder if he's a `bad one', but Mum is talking to him and holding his hands.

He looks like an animal. Something from another universe. He skin is so white, white that it looks like he might be a ghost. Even his hair is white. White like snow and glass.

"Why's your hair so white?" I ask.

"It's not white, stupid, it's blonde," he says, but his eyes are laughing at me.

It's okay. I don't mind when people laugh at me. Mum says laughing is like sunlight – the more you get, the more you grow.

So we take him home. Mum holds his hand like he's sick or somefin'. I can see him shaking from the cold and I wonder where his mama is. I want to ask if he don't have nobody to love him, but I know Mum will be cross.

"People's business is people's business," she tells me.

Mum runs him a bath – a big one like she lets me have if I'm sad. The boy pretends he doesn't want to go in, but I can see its just pretend. And while he is making small splashing noises, Mum asks me to find him some clothes.

I don't know which ones to get, so I find the new corduroys and my best transformers hoodie. I want him to feel nice after he has felt horrible.

"Mama?" I ask, but we can hear the boy splashing out of the bath and she smiles at me, stretching her arm and the clothes around the door.

The boy doesn't talk much. He says "thank you" when Mum gives him apple and custard and nods when I ask if he wants to play.

I tell him about school and my friends and what I like to watch on TV, but he doesn't say 'nuffing, just nods sometimes and throws the dice.

He has hands like spiders. The fingers are long and white and there are sore places on the knuckles. I ask him if he has eczema, because Jaydon at school has eczema and has to have a special cream. The spiders curl up and he tucks them under his arms when it isn't his turn.

I'm so busy talking that I don't hear his mama calling. The first I know, Mum is taking him by the hand. She's got his stuff in a Tesco bag and she hands it to him while she calls to someone outside the open door.

The boy's back goes hard under the transformer hoodie. His white head droops, like all the energy has gone out of him, but he goes, the plastic bag rustling against his legs as he moves. The sound makes me feel sad. I don't know why.

I peek around the edge of Mum's butt to watch him leave. There is a lady on the stairs that looks like a movie star. She has a pile of golden hair and blue on her eyes. She is wearing a very tight shirt and you can see the top of her boobs. Her words sound strange – like someone who is reading.

When she reaches out for the boy's hand, I see him twitch away and she takes his arm instead. And then he looks back at us and there is a crack in the blue of his eyes.

I want to ask why, but he dips his head and goes with the woman. I see her red nails digging into his arm and his feet stumble a little bit, but he goes.

"Mama?" I say.

Mum closes the door and leans on it. Her mouth is a straight line and she is looking past me. I check to see whether there is anything there, but it is just the kitchen, like always.

"Mama," I ask, "do you think he'll bring my hoodie back?"

Mum laughs and hugs me tighter than I need.

"Yes," she says, "I think we'll see Mercutio again."

"That's a weird name," I say.

Mercutio

Romeo goes to school every day, so I go to school too.

I am already `at school', but I don't really go and Aggie is fine with that because `they're always poking their noses in.' But Bettina said `come back any time,' so I find my school uniform and throw it on before running up the stairs.

She doesn't seem surprised to see me.

"Oh, good mornin' , darlin'," she pulls me close into the warm softness of her and hugs me like she has known me forever. I am so happy I could just burst, but I don't hug her back, just in case.

Romeo is sitting at their tiny two-man table, eating toast. It's the sort of table Aggie hates: `old people stuff', but it is perfect. Bettina takes my bag and sits me down. The toast and jam are warm and sweet and salty all at once, like the taste of tears and kisses. Romeo smiles at me.

My heart feels so full that I want to shout, but instead I say; "I can walk with Romeo to school. I do it all the time and I'm fine…"

Bettina runs her hand through my hair and a warm feeling spreads all the way down my neck.

"Maybe soon, baby. For now we'll walk together, nah?"

And we walk to school like a family. When we get to the road, Romeo's hand slips into mine and we link like a chain: Bettina, Romeo and Me.

I am so happy that I shout out answers in the classroom and Miss Brown frowns and reminds me of my manners. I'm not sure she knows who I am, so I keep shouting answers until lunch time when I can run to Romeo across the playground.

I feel so happy, I think I could just explode when I see that he is looking for me. He waves and I wave back, like soldiers finding each other on a battlefield. I don't remember if anyone ever waved to me before, but even if they did, Romeo's wave is better.

He is like sunshine. Everything about him is warm: his skin, his eyes, his smile. It's like he swallowed a chunk of light and warmth and it's lighting him up from inside.

He grins to see me. "Hey, Merc!"

Merc! My heart feels like it will burst. There is something new in me. I feel bigger.

<u>Dion</u>

I hate it all. This crap school, this crap neighbourhood, these crap kids. The whole thing is crap. I never wanted to live here and now I'm alone in a crap cold playground, surrounded by a bunch of idiots

Dad says this place is full of immigrants and other deviants. I asked him what a deviant was, but he said he'd tell me another time. Like I'm a little kid or sumfin'.

I bet that little kid over by the fence is an immigrant AND a deviant. What's he got to be so happy about – some loser family and no home to go to. Idiot. I bet he doesn't even know how crap his life is.

When Mum stuffed off, Dad said this place was the only option. So here we are, back living with Nan in her flat that smells like old people and this pants school. It's nothing like my old school. Nothing is like it was.

I wonder if Jack and Ben and Ollie miss me.

Suddenly, I feel proper bad, like I'm gonna cry or sumfin'.

Some little kid pelts past me, heading over to that other stupid kid. His hair is so white, I have to look again to check it's real.

"Hey Mark!" the black kid calls. I want to hit him, I hate him so bad. But I just look. I look at the kid with the white hair running over to the black kid – at how they are laughing with each other. My stomach hurts.

Out of the corner of my eye, I can see the playground supervisor homing in like one of those rockets dad says detect heat. I don't want to talk to her, I don't want some ideas about who I should play with. I dodge round the corner and make a break for the toilets before she can get to me. I go to the cubicle that's furthest from the door and lock it. It proper stinks, but I reckon I can take it until the end of lunchtime. I sit on the toilet and pull my feet up – that way nobody can find me. Seen it in a movie.

Mum used to take us to movies. Dad says they're a rip off.

At least I have Kevin. That's my cousin Kev - and his mates. With Dad working all the time, and me having no mates of my own, I'd be stuck with Nan. But Kev has lived here all his life and he lets me hang with him on the streets.

The streets are cool. People think we just do nuffin' when we are hangin' , but actually we're talking and checking people out, right? Some of Kev's friends tried sayin' I shouldn't be out there cos I'm too young, but when one of them beefed about it too much, Kev smacked him so hard, his nose split. It was proper funny! There was blood and snot all over the kid's face and his mouth was just stuck in one big shocked 'O'. Proper funny! And now Kev's mates just nod when they see me.

 It's the only good thing about being here – Kev.

Dad looks at me all disapproving when I say I've been hangin' with Kev, but he can't really tell me not to, 'cos what's he going to do about it? He's not around and Nan, with her mobility scooter, s'not gonna hunt me down, right? I want to laugh just thinking about it – Nan like gangsta granny…

"Don't take any of Kev's money," Dad says, "and don't do any jobs for him."

But he won't tell me why not and Kev's the only one who cares enough about me to look out for me, so I reckon Kev wins.

The bell rings for the end of lunch. Thank God – my bum is getting numb and there is a wad of toilet roll on the roof that looks like it's going to come down. It sounds like there's a stampede and the door to the bathroom bangs open. Then they're all in there, shouting and carrying on like they're in some sort of flippin' market! Bunch of losers.

When I'm walking out, I kick some kid just because.

"Ow!" he yells, but I'm long gone.

<u>Romeo</u>

Everyone just calls him Mark. We try telling them that it's really Mercutio, but they forget and when I call him 'Merc' they just call him Mark.

"That's okay," he says, "I don't care. You know my name."

I never met anyone like him. He knows a lot of stuff, but he doesn't like to say. I like to say the stuff I know. Mum says I mustn't be a wise-ass, but if you know it, you should say it, right? Not Merc. He doesn't say nuffin unless he really needs to. Like everyfin is a secret just waiting for the right time.

I don't care. I like him.

When he isn't looking, I try to see what he is like. He's quick, like a cat and he knows when someone is too close. He sort-of flickers. Doesn't jump or nuffin – just sort of flickers and is out of the way. Like a ghost. He's really white too – not like other white people white – white like milk. Or a ghost. Maybe a ghost that's come alive.

Any-ways, he can't really be a ghost 'cos everyone can see him and he can play footie. And mum can give him hugs. You can't hug a ghost, can you?

He's got this way of looking at people, 'specially grown ups, like he is x-raying them quick before they say anything. Not me. When he looks at me and mum, his eyes are all different: open, like the sky.

Mostly his eyes are like ice. My friend Ralph doesn't like him. Says he's weird. But I tell Ralph he's weird too and now he doesn't want to play anymore.

It's okay. I'll play with him if he wants to – as long as he plays with Merc too.

The bell rings for the end of lunch and the others run off. It's just Merc and me for about half a second before Mrs Waites starts yelling: `C'mon boys! Back to class!'.

"See you after school – at the gate!" I shout as we start to run.

He has a really good smile when he uses it.

***

Across the hall, the giggles have turned to whispers. Something smashes and he hears Aggie swear, but it is a muted swearing, followed by snuffling, that stretches out into snoring.

He waits. He isn't sure what he is waiting for. Something.

There is an ache deep in his belly – a longing for what once was. For the simplicity of childhood where things just happen and no figuring out is needed - when friendship solves everything.

Below in the street a car door slams loud against the muted night and voices call out to each other, the words metallic and indistinct against the dark.

When the idea comes to him, the only paper he can find is in the back of an exercise book, wrinkled from being shoved too roughly into a bag. He tears it carefully, watching the paper bleed away from the staples, obedient to the pull of his thumb. Somewhere inside something tears too and his throat tightens against a sob.

He can't find a pen and the pencil scratches unnaturally loud against the silence, like secret chanting – wishes made real.

'Dear Bettina...' he begins and he is glad that it is pencil, because the tears fall across the words, pitting the paper.

WHEN

<u>Mercutio</u>

It's our routine. I run up the stairs and barge straight in – I don't even knock any more.

"Hooo, Mercutio! How do you know I'm not in my underwear!" Bettina laughs. It's the same thing she says every day before she pulls me close for a cuddle and an inspection. I hug her back and stand still when she combs my hair with her fingers. I want to purr like a cat, but I just smile at her instead.

She wipes my face and sits me down opposite Romeo at the little table, like we are brothers.

If we were brothers, I'd be the big brother. Romeo has done some growing, but he's still only up to my eyes.

Doesn't matter.

I look across the table and we smile at each other. He eats toast like it is a lobster or something really expensive and delicious, concentrating on each bite and chewing as if there's some brilliant toasty flavour no-one else knows about.

I love watching him eat toast. Somehow it makes my toast taste better too.

"C'mon now, boys, time to get yourselves off," Bettina is tucking sandwich boxes into both our bags. She never once asked me if I need lunch – she just makes it for me. She's been doing it for more than a year now, so it's just part of our routine.

"Look after each other!" she calls as she lets us out and we jump down the stairs two at a time, trying to make as much noise as we can.

School is only two blocks away, but we're late and so we run like mad things down the pavement, our bags banging on our backs and our feet slapping hard. Romeo runs with his head down, arms pumping, but he never beats me – I'm always faster. And I pay more attention.

I see the group of big kids and swerve to avoid them.

Romeo runs straight into the biggest one.

"Ooof," the kid stumbles and almost falls. He grabs at Romeo, catching him by the arm.

"Sorry! Sorry!," Romeo manages between breaths ," I was going so fast, I didn't see you! Sorry! Are you okay?"

I've stopped to watch. I don't trust other people, especially not groups of other people. Groups make people mean. Aggie is always worse when she has someone with her.

"He's okay!" I call. "C'mon, we're late."

But I can see the big kids have other plans. The one Romeo ran into grips his arm tighter. He is tall and spotty – and there is something mean in his eyes.

"Hang on, hang on…" he starts.

I see him look sideways at his friends to make sure they are watching. There's a funny slow sickness that starts to grow in my throat - something in his look reminds me of Aggie when she wants to hurt me.

 I take Romeo's hand and pull him.

"C'mon, " I say.

"Hang on, hang on…" says the boy and he holds Romeo's arm tighter. Romeo's eyes are round and scared.

One of the friends opens Romeo's backpack and fishes out his lunch.

"Ooooh," he says, "and what has mummy made for us today?"

Romeo watches him, mesmerised.

"Let him go," I say, "we're late for school."

Spotty boy looks at me as though I have just appeared.

"And, erm, who are you?"

I hit him then: smack my fist between his eyes so that his nose explodes in a gush of blood and he drops Romeo's arm.

"Run!" I yell, but Romeo is standing, stuck, his eyes wide and his face covered with Spotty Boy blood.

"C'mon!" I grab at his arm, but Spotty's friend is already hitting me.

He is bigger than me and hits me hard on the side of the head before I can dodge. It's like being hit with a frying pan and my ears ring. But I live with Aggie, so I've done this before. The trick is to stay on your feet.

He tries again, but I am too quick and I bite down on the hand, clenching my teeth until I feel the skin pop. He is screaming and hitting me with his other fist, but I cling on and keep my head down. His blood is like metal in my mouth.

From far away I hear someone shouting. It's a man's voice.

"Oi! I'm calling the police!"

I'm shaken off and there's a little while when I am so dizzy that my eyes won't stop spinning. I keep my head down and the sound of running feet is like the soundtrack of the tarmac. There is blood dripping onto the grey, and I wonder if it is mine.

Romeo!

For a minute I think he is hurt and I feel sick, but then I see it is only Spotty Boy's blood and Romeo is standing, pressed against the railings, his school bag clutched tight to his chest. His eyes are huge and dark and when he looks at me, he starts to cry. Its silent. The tears just tumble out of his eyes.

"It's okay," I say, but it comes out funny.

The man is trying to look at me without touching.

"Can I take you kids somewhere?" he asks, but I shake my head.

"No, s'okay," I manage, and this time it sounds like words. "We'll go home."

I take Romeo's hand. He is shaking. His fingers curl around mine and we stand for a moment. I feel his grip tighten, as if he is telling me something that words can't. Then he picks up my bag.

"Thanks, Mister," he says, "we'll go home. My Mum is home."

<u>Romeo</u>

It's my fault. I ran into that kid and made him angry. I would have let them have my lunch. I don't care. But he won't let me go and Merc hits him.

All the time he is fighting, Merc says nuffin. The big kids are shouting and screaming and swearing, but Merc says nuffin.

And me? I can't do nuffin. I watch because I can't do nuffin. I don't know how to help. I just watch. The kid is hitting Merc as hard as he can – proper tryin' to kill him and Merc's head is down. There is blood everywhere and I can't do a single thing.

Then the boys run and there's a man and Merc is holding my hand. His spider hand is like wire on mine. His hair is full of blood and his eye is swelling up. He looks at me.

"s'okay," he says.

I don't know what to feel, I'm all jumbly inside, so I pick up his bag and walk close to him all the way home. I think about holding his arm, having him lean on me y' know, like if someone breaks a leg, but he doesn't need me to hold him up. I can feel it, walking home with him – somehow he is holding us both up.

Mum is hoovering when we get home and so we leave blood marks on the door when we knock.

"Oh my God!" she says when she opens it. Her hands are on my face first. She is wiping off the blood and looking for an injury, her breath is fast and hot against my skin. I can feel her heart thumping in her fingertips.

"Not me, Mum."

Merc just stands there. His eye has swollen shut.

Mum doesn't ask what happened. She sends me for a bowl and a cloth and wipes the blood off Merc's face. He doesn't make a sound.

"I don't think it's too bad, but we might need to go to the doctor just in case," she says at last.

Merc shakes his head.

"Go on," Mum says to me, "go get a bag of peas and let's see if we can stop the swelling."

While I rummage around in the freezer looking for peas, I hear her talking all soft-soft, her voice like treacle. I know it won't work. If Merc says he's not going to the doctor, then he's not.

Mum leaves us to make hot chocolate, her face all worried. I hold the bag of peas on Merc's eye. I don't know how it's supposed to help his eye and my hand is getting cold. I feel like there is something big I need to say, but the words won't come.

"Does your eye hurt," I ask.

He nods.

"You fought like a lion," I start to say and Merc looks up at me, making me drop the peas. His face is all tight, like he wants to cry.

"Will you still be my friend?" It is a whisper.

He is the best friend I have ever had. I want to say it, but it sounds naff.

"Yes."

I pick up the bag of peas and hold it on his eye. I smile and try to make him feel what is in my heart.

When Mum brings us the hot chocolate, little drops keep falling into his cup, but he won't look up, so maybe it's the peas.

<u>Dion</u>

I feel like I have a secret when I go out to lunch. Kev told me that some kids from his school got beaten up. He was laughing.

"They tried to say it was a gang, but one of them messed up – said it was a little albino kid. Just one!"

He was proper tickled. I laughed too – it's nice when someone unexpected wins. Dad says none of us can do a damn thing because the government are all a bunch of slackers, just letting in all those immigrants who take our jobs and don't even speak English. The way dad talks, everything is always shit. So its nice when a little kid wins.

I wonder if an albino is an immigrant.

I tried asking Nan when I got in last night, but she thought I was asking what an Albanian is, so I had to sit through an hour of the Atlas that smells like someone was sick in it in 1972. And I'm pretty sure Kev wasn't talking about an Albanian.

I've kept the secret all morning, waiting to tell Will. It's a cool bit of news, and I don't need to say anything about an albino.

The usual bunch of kids are playing over by the fence. That annoying black kid is all quiet today. Makes a change from all that laughing – like a flippin' wind-up toy! Not that his buddies seem to notice. They've got their own proper little gang now. Bunch of losers. Think they're so important. I can't wait to leave this stupid school and hang out with kids that act their age. Just four more months.

Will is over in a corner, gossiping to Levi. It makes me cross that he didn't wait for me outside the canteen – he knows that stupid dinner lady always makes me eat my fruit. Miserable old cow. And I'm supposed to be his friend - but I guess Levi's okay.

"Whazzup?" I ask.

Will puts out his fist and we bump. Levi too.

"Levi says that Year 4 boy beat up some high school kids."

Will blurts it out and jacks my news.

"What boy?"

Levi scans the playground and points: "that one!"

He is pointing at the white-haired kid who is hanging out with the kids by the fence.

"Nah!" I say, "my cousin said the kid who beat them up was an albino."

I can see that Will doesn't know what to say, but Levi frowns.

"Well, that kid is really pale. Maybe he's an albino...."

I squint across to the group by the fence. The boy has his back to us, but his hair really is white – like snow or paper. Is that what an albino looks like?

I want to shrug and say nah, no way, but then the kid turns around and I can see that there's a bruise down one side of his face and he has a black eye.

"Sheesh!" says Will.

Romeo

We didn't tell no-one what happened. Nobody, NO –
BOD - EY! Not even Ben who is my favourite friend
after Merc. But people are talking all the time. When it
first happened, the teachers were proper concerned, but
Merc said he fell off a skateboard and nobody can
prove nuffin else – even if they try. But, man, they
tried! They kept on and on asking me if I knew what
happened, but I said I didn't know. Its Merc's secret
and he's my friend.

His face is getting better now, which is good, because
first, everybody, everywhere was like: "OMG, what
happened to your face?" and then "Hey Rom, what
happened to his face?" over and over and over… So it's
good it's getting better.

I look at him carefully as we go round and round on the
round-about. His white hair covers his face like a sheet
when it blows. He doesn't mind if I stare. Sometimes
he looks up and his eyes smile at me. We are in the
playground down by our block. Mum says it needs a
good lick of paint and it only has those baby swings
that kids go in when they would fall off normal ones.
Tayo tried to get in one last week and got stuck. It was
proper funny trying to get him out. Raj tried tipping
him upside down, but all that did was make him hit his
head. We was laughing so much that we couldn't help
him. Then Tayo needed a wee and really wanted to get
out. I was laughing so much that I needed a wee too,
but Merc climbed up behind him on the swing and sort-
of pulled him out. He does that sort of stuff, Merc. Just
sorts it out.

Mum says as long as I'm with Merc I'll be okay.

The whole gang are here: Merc, Ben, Raj and Tayo. We all live close by, but only me and Merc in our block.

Ben has a really posh name. He is really called Benjamin Harrington Oakley-Smith and his mum and dad are artists. When we want to make him mad, we call him `Harrington'. Its proper funny, 'cos Ben doesn't get mad like anyone else. His lips go really tight and his face gets redder and redder like he is going to explode. But he never does. Just gets redder and redder until he gets up and goes home, walking all stiff, like the fury has made his muscles into cement. Merc says he looks like he's got a carrot up his bum. Ben hates that too!

Ben is proper clever. He knows loads of good words and puts then together like they are just beads he can thread.

"Hey, Ben," I say when he jumps back onto the roundabout after speeding it up , "tell us a poem."

Ben thinks and I can see Merc's long fingers twisting together.

"Go on!" yells Tayo.

"This is a roundabout of our lives," Benny starts, and Raj and Tayo snort, but I don't care. I love the way Ben can say words.

"We are like prisoners," Ben says, "round and round, while the world rushes by. Round and round we go – where we will stop, who knows?"

Tayo properly laughs then: "I'll free you!" he yells and pushes Ben off the roundabout.

"Jail break!" yells Raj and all three of them run to the climbing frame.

I want to just sit and think about what Ben said. He always makes me think. I look across to Merc to see if he is thinking too. But he is watching me and there is a crack in his eyes.

"You ok?" I start to say, but he puts his head down and gets off the roundabout.

"Gotta go home," he says.

I run to catch up with him, but he won't say what's wrong.

Mercutio

It's okay that we have a gang. It's nice to hang with Raj and Tayo and Ben and we have a proper laugh. I know they like to be with Romeo more than me, but it doesn't matter. I haven't ever had four whole friends before. Its good 'cos I don't need to talk too much. I can just listen.

I like them all, I swear down I do. Just Ben gets on my nerves. He always wants to be with Romeo and he talks all the time. He's good with his words, Ben. He is the top in our whole year group for English and he is in a gifted and talented group. Like he's something special.

I hate it when Romeo asks him to say a poem.

I dunno why.

We're going round and round on the roundabout. I like it here. Going round and round makes the world disappear and I feel empty inside, like everything has just been swirled away – no Aggie, no wondering if there is food, no wondering if I can get my school shirt clean for tomorrow. Just round and round with my mates.

Then Romeo asks Ben for a poem.

Ben talks some sort of rubbish about prisoners, his voice all sing-songy like he's on the stage or something. Tayo is laughing and Raj snorts so hard that snot comes out. But Romeo is looking at Ben like he's some sort of hero. His eyes are on Ben's face and he is smiling all over.

I don't know what happens. My heart grows like a brick inside me and feels so heavy, I want to choke. I want to smash Ben.

I don't know why my hands are shaking. I pick up my bag and go home. I want to run, but my whole body feels too heavy.

My heart hurts.

<u>Dion</u>

I can see them from here on the corner, but they can't see me – which is cool. I'm not really watching them any-ways, just waiting for Kev to turn up. Nan was on a proper one this afternoon. She saw something on telly about how inner-city kids are behind in education and she wanted to get proper stuck into homework. I told her I had a club and got outta there as fast as I could. I can't wait to get to Secondary. Kev reckons I'll like it 'cos its got proper Science and PE and clubs every afternoon.

"None of that stupid little kid stuff," he said. Which is good, 'cos I've proper had enough.

The kids are laughing so hard they can hardly run to the climbing frame.

The black kid and the pale kid are still on the roundabout. Just going round and round, slower and slower.

I don't think he's really an albino. Dad showed me pictures and he doesn't look like that.

I told dad I needed to know for school.

"Bloody stupid stuff you have to learn for school," dad said. "What's the point of that, then?"

And Nan got started on the Albanian again. She'd been reading the newspaper about people coming to settle in the UK and listed off the numbers and countries.

"And Albanians!" she said and dad looked at her like he needed another drink.

Nah - that kid's just pale. And skinny. He's so skinny I can't imagine how he could beat anyone up. I try to imagine him hitting someone and it just looks stupid. I bet he couldn't beat me up. I imagine what it would look like if I hit him. I think about hitting him in the eye, but I dunno what colour his eyes are, so I can't really imagine it. But I bet he would cry. Stupid little kid.

He's getting up now. Leaving the playground. His back is straight and stiff and that hair is blowing in the wind like those feathers on the top of a cockatoo. The black kid is running after him, but he's not havin' it.

"Hey Bruv!" It's Kev and his mates. "What'ya lookin at?"

He looks so cool. I wish dad would let me have a jacket like that. Not this stupid fleece thing. I try pushing the sleeves up, but they're too thick.

"Nuffin." I say.

I don't want Kev to see me watching little kids like some billy no-mates and I jump off the wall before he gets there.

"So, what we doin'?"

Kev laughs and puts an arm round my shoulder. The feel of his arm is good.

"Business, little man, business."

I want to look back to see what the white-haired kid is doing, but I don't want Kev to see.

"Cool!" I say.

Mercutio

When I'm with Bettina and Romeo, I pretend they're
my family. It's like Aggie disappears. The hard eyes
and the mouth spitting at me, that hard cold stone of
dread that lies in my stomach when she's close – it all
just goes away. I love being with Bettina and Romeo.

"Just get out," Aggie says. I am half-in her doorway,
ready to run if she throws something. I want to go to
the `big park' with Bettina. I've never been to any park
other than the playpark outside the tower blocks and I
am scared Aggie will say no.

She's not properly awake and she drops the end of her
cigarette into a cider bottle on the floor. I don't think
she really hears me, because she repeats `just get out'
and I don't care. I shut the door carefully, hoping that
the noise doesn't wake her up properly. My feet are all
jumpy - I never go anywhere special and the
excitement is like wasps stinging at my bones so I can't
stand still.

"I don't have money to waste on you!" I hear her yell
after me. She is awake!

But my key and the £1 from the kitchen table are
already in my pocket and my feet are pounding up the
stairs before the front door slams. I don't care, I don't
care, I don't care – I'm going to the park with Bettina
and Romeo.

It's my first time ever on a bus, a proper red double-
decker. Bettina lets us sit up top and at the front.
There's no space for her, but she just smiles: "You go
on, boys – I have seen it before". She winks at me.

We watch London go by like we are gods, looking
down on everyone else.

I feel like someone in a movie, here in the front of a bus, high above the cars. Romeo is next to me, his face is all lit up and I can feel the warmth of Bettina in the seat behind us. I know we have sandwiches and crisps and will have a picnic when we find `a good spot.' Life is perfect. I am not Mercutio. I am Merc, son of Bettina.

When we get there, the park is all the green and trees that Bettina promised and me and Romeo run and run until we can't breathe. When we get sick of running in circles, Bettina finds a bench near the play area and we scrabble to climb the climbing frame, puffing and hoisting ourselves as high as we can.

"This is the best day ever!" says Romeo. I smile and smile and smile so that my face hurts.

There is a girl on the platform below us. Her blonde hair is up in a ponytail and she looks like she escaped from a magazine – all perfect. She is licking a lolly and she looks up at us with a scrunched nose.

"Is that lady your nanny?" she asks.

I am confused. So is Romeo.

"What lady?"

The girls waves her lolly at Bettina. That lady.

"Nah, that's mum! She's too young to be a nanny!" says Romeo. We laugh at the girl 'cos she's so stupid.

The girl scrunches her nose up and licks her lolly.

"Not a NAN – a nanny, a lady whose job it is to take you to the park."

We're still confused.

"Mum brought us to the park," says Romeo.

The girl looks from us to Bettina. She licks her lolly and looks hard at me: "where's your mum?" she says.

Suddenly the day isn't perfect anymore. Shame welds my mouth shut and I don't know where to look. My mum is at home sleeping 'cos she doesn't care what I do.

"Merc is with us," says Romeo and I find he is standing close to me, looking down at the girl with the ponytail.

She looks back at us coolly. "Why?" she says.

I don't know what to say. I just stand there, my heart beating fast and all the excitement and happiness disappearing like mist. Then Romeo puts his arm around my shoulder, standing on tip-toes so that his arm goes all the way around my neck.

"Cos we're best friends," he says matter-of-factly.

Then he nudges me and I hear him snort a little giggle.

"Where's your best friend?" he asks the girl. He pretends to look all over for the friend.

The girl stuffs the lolly in her mouth and climbs away.

"Stupid boys," she mutters and she misses her step climbing down the ladder. The lolly tumbles into the sand and she hangs, howling.

The woman who comes running looks like a bigger version of her daughter : "Oooh Cherry – Cheryloo, what's happened, darlin'…"

Romeo is laughing so that he can't stand up and he has to hang onto my legs so that he doesn't fall off the climbing frame too.

So I laugh as well. We are laughing so hard that we slip and have to hang onto the bars like monkeys. So we laugh even harder and Bettina comes over to check on us.

"You be careful, boys," she says wagging a finger at us , "no falling and breaking anything now…"

We laugh and laugh.

I wish I could just stay like this forever. With Romeo next to me.

***

He wants to write, to say something meaningful, to explain. But there are shadows in the dark and when he closes his eyes, the night comes rushing back – the running and the blood. That feeling like a rock in his stomach. Knowing that this will be a goodbye. Must be goodbye.

Part of him wishes he could go back to being a little kid. Not all of it, but some of it – the being best of friends, no matter what. The easiness of it all. Toast in the morning, snakes-and-ladders, hanging out on the roundabout. Believing that it would always be good – at least that part. When did that end? He finds himself searching: when did it end? When did the just being a kid with a best friend, end?

He puts the pencil against the paper, but the words don't come. He tries to articulate what Bettina has meant to him, but it is beyond him. There aren't words for all the sun and hope and heartache. And so he writes two lines, his spindly words spiked like a heart monitor across the page.

It is quiet, the witching hour long gone. Outside the glass of his window, the world is turning, cancelling out the day that was. Resetting. The sky is a black canvas against which satellites and aeroplanes meander like electrical faults. Pulse beats. By tomorrow, tonight will be the third page in a newspaper. Nobody will know his name. Tomorrow.

Third page unless someone dies. Another stabbing and all the politicians will be out spouting about youth violence. If someone dies it might make the front page.

The bile rises in his throat and he spits into the rubbish bin.

Not yet.

Nobody is dead yet.

Carefully he tears another page from the book.

`Romeo' he writes, but the lines lead him nowhere and all he can do is sit and look at the word: Romeo, Romeo.

"Soon," he thinks, "soon, I'll know."

His phone beeps a little distress signal and he checks the messages – nothing.

There is nothing to do but wait. He can't do anything until he knows. He has to wait. And then? He wonders what it will be like to be somewhere else. To be someone else.

THEN

<u>Mercutio</u>

When I wake up, Aggie is looking at me from the doorway. Since I turned 15 she seems to do this more and more – like I'm some sort of experiment, or something she's fattening up for dinner like the witch in Hansel and Gretal. Her dressing gown doesn't cover her properly and her thin nightie shows me more than I want to see. I want to close my eyes, but she is looking at me.

She leans her shoulder into the doorframe and takes a long pull of her cigarette. I don't like the way she looks at me. Her gaze makes my skin prick and I pull the duvet closer. The smoke comes out her nose in grey whisps.

"What?" I say, turning my face away.

"You're going to be late." She pulls on her cigarette and her eyes narrow. This early in the morning, her hair is lank and her skin sallow. She has lost some teeth and her jaw is beginning to sink. Without makeup she looks old.

"Get up," she says, her voice brittle and cold. She pushes off from the door. "Get up and get out."

She must have company coming.

I would argue, but I've played this game before. She hasn't hit me in ages now – too big I suppose – but I've lived with Aggie for a long time and she'll have some sort of revenge.

I get up, tucking the duvet around me so that I have to waddle like some sort of demented sausage roll on legs. I don't exactly push her out, but I close the door.

She snorts loudly and her scratchy nails-on-a-board laugh sounds.

"All coy now? Think you're something special, Boy? Remember that I had to wipe your backside... I know exactly what you look like."

She doesn't. She watches me all the time, but she has never seen me. Ever.

My shirt is still scrunched on the floor. I forgot to rinse it through, so it'll have to do. My clothes smell a bit, but its nearly the end of the week and I hardly notice as I pull them on. Hurry, hurry, get out before she comes back!

I have it down to a fine art – five minutes and I'm out. I don't say a goodbye – she'll know I'm gone when the door closes.

Running up the stairs to Bettina's flat is like being released. I know for certain that she will smile at me and the flat will smell of warm toast. I do it every morning. Every morning for years now and still, every morning, it's like climbing out of some sort of grave and getting into the light.

"Mornin' Lovely," Bettina says. She is ironing something and the kitchen smells like a mix of warm cotton and toast. I go to hug her and she wrinkles her nose and ruffles my hair : `"quick shower, I think!"

Romeo nods at me from across the table. My heart is full.

Home.

"Hey Merc," says Rom , " be quick, bruv – Ben is back. "

I remember then. Ben is back. It doesn't matter. Even when Romeo smiles at him, he doesn't have this – Romeo and Bettina in the morning.

"Shower!" says Bettina. I go.

<u>Ben</u>

It's bloody amazing to be back!

For some stupid reason, I'm waiting on the roundabout, spinning round and round like an idiot. I don't fit on it the same as when we were kids and the steel is making my arse numb, but it feels like the best place to meet the gang.

Romeo and Merc are first. I see the shock of Merc's hair before I see their faces. He's a head taller than Rom – but when they come down the path, they look like they are perfectly matched – like that yin and yang sign. Piano keys.

 Romeo's whole face lights up when he sees me – his grin is like a toothpaste advert and his eyes proper shine. I can't help but grin back. His arms are wide open:

"Hey, Benny! Good to see you, bruv! No more stupid elitist Art school for you!"

Merc looks happy to see me – as happy as he ever looks. His mouth doesn't smile, but his eyes aren't hard. We bump fists and he nods at me. It's about as warm as Merc gets.

"So you're back." He says.

Not that I wasn't back – I just wasn't back-back. All the hard work to win a place at Art School – all the long bus rides and late nights. All that crap. And in the end, Art just doesn't do it for me anymore. I don't want to be like Banksy – not that I've got anything against Banksy. Banksy is great. But Art School is all like : `you have to be original ; hey take inspiration from Turner. Well, that's not very Turner…And other crap.'

And I missed my mates – even Merc. The guys at Art school are so focussed on making it big that everything else disappears. Not this bunch! I'm glad to be back – feels like I'm proper alive here in this shitty little park in between the towers. Feels like real life.

"Yeah," I say, "back to this dump. Back to the gang."

Raj and Tayo are calling from the corner: "Yoh! Is that Harrington I see!"

And then we're all a bundle of back slaps and swearing. It's so good to be back!

We're all taller and bigger (and poor Tayo is quite a bit spottier), but it just feels so normal to be walking to school with this bunch of idiots again.

Like always, Romeo is in the middle. Like a short campfire, I suppose, with us pilgrims on either side of him. Proper golden boy, our Rom.

"Hey, Man," he says, a swagger in his walk and his voice , "look at us! Jus' like the `ole days, Boyyakka!" He snaps his fingers and we all grin. Romeo's `gangsta' is almost polite.

We're just a block from school, bowling along and laughing like fools at the banter, when Merc goes all stiff, like suddenly there's steel rods in his shoulders and arms. He doesn't stop that long sloping walk – doesn't even miss a step – but his grip gets tight on his bag strap and his head goes down. A wall of cold comes off him.

"Oh, for ffs's sake ," I hear him mutter, more to himself than us.

Ahead of us, some random blokes are blocking the footway. The one in the middle, an ugly mug with acne scars and a slash across his cheek is eying Merc.

"Oi!" he yells, stepping forward as if he expects us to stop.

Romeo, Tayo and Raj falter, but Merc keeps on, not a break in his stride.

"Who's this lot?" I mutter to Romeo.

"Crap," he says. His eyes are big and his mouth has fallen open. An open book, Romeo. It's clear that there's trouble here.

Meanwhile Merc is pulling opposite Spotty Slashface.

"Oi!" says Slashface. "I know you. Think you're too big for a hiding? Hey! You!"

Anyone can see that Merc is coiled and dangerous, like lightning, but Slashface has his gang at his back and must feel safe.

Merc makes to go around him and he grabs at Merc's arm.

My heart jumps into my throat. Don't get me wrong, I can handle myself, but the Art School guys aren't much into physical fighting and I don't like the look of this lot.

Then, before I can even figure out a plan, things get proper weird.

Romeo swings his bag to the ground and steps forward, his arms wide like he is calming a rabid dog.

"Hey, whoa," he says, all cheerful and calm-like, "hey, man, what's the problem?"

"And I know you!" says Slashface. He is spitting the words and his eyes are narrow and mean. It would be funny if it was on youtube, but it's not. Because he looks proper pissed – and mean, like he wants to kill Merc and now Romeo too.

Merc is cool - he has shrugged Slashface off and looks like he might walk away, but Romeo has gone mad and is striking up a conversation. None of us can move – all afraid to tip the balance.

"You're the cry-baby," Slashface taunts, sticking his face into Romeo's, "standing on the side while your mate gets a pelting…" His cronies snigger behind him.

"Hey," says Romeo, all calm and I wonder for a moment if he is on drugs , "hey – that was a long time ago…"

Raj, Tayo and me just stand – we don't know what they're on about, but it isn't looking good. Slashface and his mates look like they want blood.

Then Romeo pats Slashface on the shoulder, all friendly and familiar: "water under the bridge, Bruv…"

He is smiling his best Romeo smile, warm and friendly, an open book.

We can't believe it. Neither can Slashface.

His fist lands square on Rom's nose, blood popping as he knocks him backwards and down.

It's all a bit mad after that.

<u>Mercutio</u>

Aggie says a bad smell hangs around forever.

It's been years – but I know him the minute I see him. Spotty, although he's not so Spotty anymore and someone has tagged his face. Grown, but the same. I know he knows me too.

"Oi!" he yells.

I keep my head down and keep walking, but then he grabs at me, his fingers hard on my upper arm.

"Oi!"

I know I can take him, but I don't want to. I just want to walk away.

Then flippin' Romeo is there like some sort of idiot side-kick. He has his arms wide like a lion-tamer and is talking all soft and calm.

I can't believe it and neither can Spotty-not-Spotty. He drops his hand from my arm so that he can concentrate on the weird event that is Romeo. Then Romeo pats him. Just friendly-like on his shoulder, like he's making friends with a dog or something.

It would be funny if Spotty had a sense of humour. For about half a second he is frozen in the shock of it all, then he hits Romeo.

Romeo goes down, his eyes big and surprised, blood spurting from his nose. His eyes flick up at me like they did when we were kids: "Merc?"

He doesn't have to ask. We are already stuck in, kicking and grunting and doing damage wherever we can. It's like deja-vu as Spotty's fist smashes home and

I bite hard at the knuckles and tear skin. I get his fingers and bend them back as far as they will go.

Spotty is screaming, but that doesn't bother me and I keep my head down, ramming at him until he hits the floor, one arm pinned underneath him. He keeps bashing at my head with his other fist and trying to shake me off, but I hang on and slug at his ribs until Ben is pulling at me.

"Merc!"

I let go. Spotty looks like shit, but so do we.

We've all been properly pummelled. My left eye is already swelling shut and I know my face is a mess. Raj has lost a tooth and Ben's tie is ripped clean in half, but we hang on each other and laugh as Spotty and his boys back off.

"You fuckers!" Spotty manages. He is holding his hand, but he spits venom. "I'll get you!" He throws the words at me as his boys hustle him away.

Raj flips him the bird and we laugh and laugh.

"For flipp's sake, Rom," Tayo manages at last, "you gotta know your audience!"

And then we laugh so hard that we can't stand and so we bunk off to the playground. We're in too much of a mess for school any-way. For about half a second I wonder what Ben's parents are going to think about his decision to change school.

"Hey, welcome back, mate," says Raj, throwing an arm around Ben's shoulder. Ben laughs, and his eyes flicker from me to Rom. Cautious Ben – always trying to understand.

Romeo is grinning, but somewhere something has changed. He looks over his shoulder at the corner that Spotty and gang disappeared around. Maybe he doesn't believe that good people win any more. I want to say that I've known it for a long time.

We sit on the roundabout and Tayo finds us a fag to share. My face is stinging and my shirt is torn. Rom sits with his shoulder against mine, the feel of his heat spreading through me.

"Sorry, Merc," he says, so quietly that nobody else can hear.

I'm not sorry.

I suddenly want to hold his hand so badly that it's as if I'm being pulled by a magnet. I want it to be just me and him.

Romeo.

"No worries," I say and I force myself to move away from him and head home, even though I know Aggie will be there.

I don't run, but I don't turn around when they call.

<u>Dion</u>

Tim Ashby. That's his name. He's got a gang and all - Tim Ashby's gang. They've got a name, but I don't know what it is. Bet it's bloody stupid, any-way. Tim's got some street-cred from being knifed in the face by an uptown gang. Kev says he's small potatoes, but we all know that he's mean, in a sneaky sort of way.

I'm just waiting to finish my smoke, just outta sight of the school gate when I see it all kick off.

Tim Ashby's an arse. This isn't even his patch, so I dunno what he's doing here. He's been cut, so he thinks he's proper hard. Arsehole. He should know what mean looks like – but he takes on that white-haired kid. Idiot. I don't fight, but I can spot a fighter and that kid looks like he was born to kick Tim Ashby's head in.

I watch him. I watch them. But mostly I watch him.

There is something, something I can't put my finger on. Like heat without heat. Like focus without wanting to be focussed. Like a tornado, I suppose. It smashes like it intends to – but maybe it didn't. Tim Ashby looks stupid fighting him.

Then they're done. Tim Ashby's boys don't exactly run, but I can see they got smashed.

The white-haired kid and his mates fall all over each other.

Their laughter carries to the corner and I can see how the shorter kid looks up at his mate. I think I see something, but then:

"Are you planning on coming in some time, Dion?"

It's Mr Ells at the gate. He's waiting to lock. He can't
see the others – they're too far round the corner.

I drop my butt and jog in.

"Sorry, Mr Ells, problems at home…"

He says something behind me, but I'm jogging into the
crowds. I look out for the white-haired boy, even
though I know he's not here.

<u>Romeo</u>

It's flippin' good to have the gang back together again! I missed having Benny around – someone for Merc to bounce off. Mum says Merc is a `genuine good kid', but trouble is his shadow.

"Probably will always be," she said one night when he went off home. She watched him go like she wanted to pull him back. I still don't see what she sees, why she gets all sad when he heads home.

Any-way, I guess she's right, 'cos no matter what Merc does, or doesn't do, trouble just wants to bite at him. I feel bad for him. There he is, looking out for me all the time and there trouble is, just waiting to ambush him.

It's like that fight on the way to school. We were all in it, but the only person anyone seems to remember is Merc. Every idiot in the school wants to take him on. I keep telling them that it wasn't just him, but people reckon I'm jealous of the attention. No flippin' way! Who wants that attention? Merc can't hang in the playground without some smart arse testing him out. There's always someone who `accidently' bashes him. Lucky Merc doesn't give a crap what people think.

There's this sixth-former, Dion somebody. He's like first team club footie or something and he's proper full of himself. Swaggers around with his mates. He's been watching Merc and all – seen him watching him for ages now. Pretends he isn't, but he always is. Any-ways, since the fight, he's been making moves. Small stuff - `accidental' stuff – but it's getting worse. Like he wants Merc to take the bait.

It's the second half of lunch and we've got the sunny corner at the edge of the basketball court when Dion's mate kicks a ball over. Straight at us. Tayo kicks it back, but the idiot kicks it back again, like he's aiming at us or sumfin'.

Ben punts it back: "hey, mate, there's a whole court…"

The Dion bloke picks up the ball.

"What'ya say?" He should be talking to Ben, but he's talking to Merc.

"Just that there's a whole court," says Ben.

Dion doesn't look at him, but he bounces the ball so that it hits the fence by our heads. He's watching Merc.

Merc doesn't say a word, he just walks away. We follow. Not bothering Dion at all. But then him and his mates are playing footie around us and Dion crashes into Merc, knocking him down.

He holds up his hands, but it is a long second before the words come out: "sorry, mate. You should look where you're going."

Ben is helping Merc up. We're all waiting to see what will happen, including Dion the Dickhead. But Merc does nothing. He doesn't even look at Dion as he walks away.

"Arsehole," says Tayo. But he says it quietly.

We follow Merc off the court. Dion's mates are having a good giggle at us, but I can see that Dion kid isn't really laughing along – he's just making the sounds. He's watching Merc as he goes, like he's trying to figure something out.

Then he sees me watching.

"What you looking at?"

I drop my eyes. I'm not afraid of Dion, but I don't want trouble and I know Merc will be there if Dion tries it on. There's something about Dion. Not just his attitude. There's something there that I don't trust. Mum says you can always see a bad dog. It's in the way that it looks at you, as if its hiding something. It can wag its tail and lick you, but the eyes will flicker over you. Dion looks like that. Big first team footie player, but there's something hiding behind that man-bun and cockiness. Something he's not letting the world see.

Merc is holding back from the others, but when I catch up with them, they're way out on the edge of the field. There's a group of girls under the oak tree. I can hear them laughing all high and false-like. They're worse than Dion and his mates, 'cos you never know what they're thinking. They all look the same – straightened hair and skirts rolled up. In a group, they're flippin' scary!

 As I catch up with the gang, the girls start to rag us:

"Hiya, Ben!" They all love Ben. Proper movie-star material and all. He waves back, cool as you like. Ben isn't scared of girls, even in a pack.

"Hiya, Tayo!" Tayo just about blows up he blushes so hard. He tries to wave, but he looks like a stuck robot, he is so stiff and awkward – and the girls laugh so that some of them have to fall over.

Raj is right up there: "Hey, girls!" But they ignore him. It's no fun ragging someone who doesn't bite. One of them wolf-whistles and they all laugh.

"Hiya, Mark!" Its Cheryl or Cherry, or something. Everyone calls him that – I guess `Mercutio' was lost in the wash a bit. The other girls echo her: "Hi-ya, Mark!"

Cheryl/Cherry has taken off her school tie and her shirt is undone enough to see the tops of her boobs. They're quite big boobs - no wonder Tayo is in meltdown.

Merc keeps walking. He half-waves, but he doesn't look their way. Ben and Raj peel off towards the girls.

"Hey Mark," Cheryl/ Cherry calls loudly, "come sit with us too."

Merc doesn't stop. The girls call again. He looks at me and there's a flicker of something in his eyes. I know he doesn't want to go anywhere near them.

"Yoo-hoo!" Cheryl/Cherry calls, "bring Romeo too!"

Merc's head is down and he is walking a bit faster. The back of his neck is getting all red – embarrassed or angry, I can't tell.

"Nah!" I yell back, "we got somefin' to do!"

He's my mate. My best mate.

I walk on and Merc walks with me.

Behind us, Tayo is lost, then he takes his chances and joins Ben. I hear the girls laughing their heads off.

"Chicken!" one yells after us.

It's just words. Me and Merc walk away. I look to see if I can understand, but his shutters are down. Its ok. About time I saved him and all.

<u>Mercutio</u>

The problem with the world is that it is too full of people who want a piece of you. If you don't give it, then they think they can just take it.

I can handle the Dions. They're easy. It's the Aggies that are the problem.

Not that I've got anything against girls. Bettina's a girl and I love her.

But so is Aggie.

I can see how it's going to end. All that straightened hair and eye-liner getting old and mean like Aggie. I can't look at them without seeing Aggie. I know it's not logical or true, but when they look at me, I feel them weighing me up, like Aggie. Like something they want a piece of.

When Cheryl calls, I want to be cool like Ben, really, I do. But I can't. I don't want to talk to them, I just want them to leave me alone.

"Maa-rk, come sit with us."

Why? What could she want from me? I feel Aggie looking at me, judging me, seeing where she can get under my skin. Make me small.

Cheryl's awful wheedling tone curls into my guts and I just want to run away – but we all know what would happen if I did that on a school playground. Everyone's watching. Waiting for failure. So I don't look, just walk. Rom says something next to me, but I can't hear him.

I just walk. My back prickles with sweat I don't want them to see.

I feel like a coward, but they don't own me. Same as Aggies doesn't own me.

Except I know she does. She owns every minute of every day that I pretend home is like every other home, that my mum is like a real mum. And every moment I am home is a cat and mouse game on how to avoid Aggie. How to avoid mentioning Aggie. How to avoid thinking about Aggie. And she is always there.

Every part of me wants to leave her behind. To walk away, like I can walk away from the girls on the field.

But I can't. I am fifteen.

And here I have Romeo and Bettina and even the tiniest thought of leaving them breaks my heart.

When the girls call me out, I think it's the sound of Aggie that makes me want to run.

<u>Ben</u>

Rom and Merc walk away. A unit.

Then Cheryl is whinging: "Hey, Be-en…."

She is twisting her hair around her finger and looking down. Her mouth has bunched into a strange little pout like a cat's backside and her voice has taken on a baby-ish tone. Coquettish, I think is what it is called. I want to laugh and I can see Tayo is going to put his foot in it because his eyes haven't been able to move from where they are glued to Cheryl's boobs. Not that she seems to mind. I see her sneak a little side glance to check he is looking.

Her friends seem to have clustered closer to her. One has her arm around her waist.

"Why doesn't your friend like me?" She flickers her lashes as if about to cry. A bit full-on, but that's Cheryl for you.

I shrug. I don't know.

Genuinely – I don't know. He's been my mate for years now and I don't know. Come to think of it, I don't know anything about him. Never seen where he lives – I mean, I know where he lives, but I've never even been to the front door. Never met his mum. Never talked about a dad or what he wants to do after school.

It's weird. Why don't I know? I wonder if Rom knows. I make a mental note to ask.

Then Lily is playing with my hair.

"He should be more friendly – like you," she says.

It's easy to smile. I like Lily.

"Maybe we need to find Romeo a girlfriend," says Lily, "then Mark would be more normal too…"

I don't know why that suggestion sounds wrong. I can't imagine someone being between Merc and Rom. It just sounds weird, but I can't think why.

"Yeah, maybe," I say and Lily puts her arms around my neck and leans her head over my shoulder.

"Definitely," she says.

We're having a laugh over some video when the bell rings. I think a bit about the mystery of Merc, but there's stuff to do.

Besides, Rom is with him – he'll be okay.

<u>Mercutio</u>

The girls have made me feel jumpy. I've had a sick feeling in my gut all afternoon and turns out I'm not wrong.

They catch up with us after school. Cheryl and her gang. Tayo and Raj aren't with us – some club. Ben is in with a teacher discussing something ground-breaking and me and Rom hang around the gate waiting for him. I feel all antsy, but I can't leave Romeo, not after what happened with Spotty – twice.

The sky has clouded over and the afternoon is getting dark. The wind starts to pick up. It's been a shit day and now we're going to get rained on while waiting for Lord Ben. I just want to get home. Well, home to Bettina's. Home-home would make the day a bit shitter, but I don't say that aloud.

"C'mon, hurry up!" we call to Ben when he finally saunters out of the main doors, success written all over him like he's been stamped from birth. A tin-hard thought sneaks into my head like a bullet - he will never be like me and I will never be like him. Ben will win and I won't. But the wind is kicking up, so I let it go. It's not Ben's fault.

The girls are in a cluster just round the corner. They are jabbering like magpies, their skirts blowing up in the wind so that they shriek and clutch at them. I want to cross the road, but someone spots us and it's like an invisible signal passes between them.

The group parts and reforms around us, like one of those clouds of starlings. It's all chatter and giggling. I keep my head down and keep walking.

Bloody Ben has slowed down. Lording it. Smiling.
He's holding Lily's hand and telling his audience about
some artist. Rom is listening, slowing his pace too.
Everyone is smiling at bloody Ben.

Sometimes I bloody hate him.

"I gotta get home," I start to say.

Then Cheryl is there.

"Hey, Mark," she says. The words are light, but her
eyes are watching me. They're quick and bright.
Thief's eyes. Her friends giggle.

"Hey, Cheryl," says Ben, all friendly and charming.
But Cheryl barely flicks her eyes at him. She is homing
in. Before I can get away, she steps in front of me so
that I can't walk forward.

"Hey, Mark." I can smell her cherry lip gloss she is so
close.

"Hey, Cheryl." I try to dodge around her, but she has a
plan and puts a hand on my chest.

"Hey, c'mon, I don't bite," she's smiling now, looking
up at me through lashes that don't look real. Her friends
are giggling. Ben doesn't stop talking. He hasn't
noticed.

I don't know what to do. I can feel my ears getting hot.

"C'mon girls, we gotta get home. It's my mum's
birthday." Romeo is lying, but it strikes a chord.

"Oh well…" Cheryl looks like she is going to give up.
She looks down at her hand on my chest. I look too.
The fingers are spread and her painted nails are a bit
chewed.

"See ya," I start to say, but then she kisses me. Just stands on her toes and kisses me right on the mouth, so that the sticky lip gloss stays like glue.

There is a little gasp and a titter runs through the girls. I want to push her away, but I don't know what to do.

"Hey!" says Rom. Ben has actually shut up.

A rage is building in my throat like a lump of sick. Cheryl is smiling up at me like she's won something.

"I didn't say you could," I manage.

Cheryl is grinning, all teeth and spider-lashes.

"Oh, Mark," she giggles and turns to her friends.

"I didn't say you could." This time I push past her so that her shoulder connects with my schoolbag.

"Ouch!" she yells after me. "You mug!"

But I keep walking. I don't know where Romeo and Ben are. My ears are burning and the taste of cherry is clogging my throat.

I didn't say she could.

And then Aggie is on the stairway, snogging some bloke who has his hand all over her. I pretend I don't know her.

When I get to the bathroom, I throw up, but the taste of cherry is still glued to my lips.

I didn't say she could.

Outside the storm breaks and thick hard drops pelt like grit against the window.

I didn't say she could.

<u>Romeo</u>

No Merc for two days. Haven't seen him at all. Two days he hasn't come for breakfast or waited on the stairs. Two days. I dunno what to do.

It's been all over school. Turns out that Cheryl (not Cherry) is a proper cow. Mum says not to talk bad about girls, but really – Cheryl's a cow. Telling everyone that she scared Merc - proper laughing at him. Like what she did was okay because she's a girl.

"It's cos he embarrassed her," Ben tried to explain, but I just think she's a cow. Not that Merc is helping things by hiding away.

Mum doesn't know what's up.

"Mercutio sick?" she asks, but I don't know what to say. I dunno how to explain to her what happened. I dunno if she'd understand. She comes from a world where men are in charge. I don't think she'll get it.

"Dunno," I say.

She looks at me sharply.

"Rom- ay -o..." when she says my name like that I know I'm in trouble, "this is your friend…" she leaves the sentence hanging, but I know what she means, so I go downstairs and knock on his door. Somewhere inside I hear his mum calling his name. Nothing happens. I knock again, proper loud.

"What!" The door is ripped open. Merc's mum is halfway through putting on her make-up and I am suspended between knocks, a bit gobsmacked at the difference between the two sides of her face.

"Um…" I manage.

"It's you." She looks me up and down like I'm
something she'd rather not have in her doorway.

"I suppose you've come for him. Useless little toe-rag.
Sulking in his room, lazy arse that he is." She laughs,
but the words are still hard and her eyes flick like a
lizard's.

She's a bit weird, Merc's mum.

She walks away, leaving the door open. I dunno if I'm
supposed to go in. I've never been in.
The hallway is bleak, man. Blue paint is chipping in
places and there are no pictures. Not even a rug on the
floor.

"Merc?" I start. And then he's there, hair rumpled and
smelling like he hasn't had a wash in two days.

He blocks the door. Anger flows out of him like a heat
wave, but he keeps his eyes down.

"What'cha want?" he says.

"Just worried, mate…mum sent me to check on you…"

It's plain like my face he doesn't want me here. His
shoulders are stiff, his hand firmly on the door.

"Okay – so all good?"

I'm backing away when I hear my mum's voice :

"tell that boy to get himself here….or else I'll come get
him."

I hope Merc's mum hasn't heard. Merc seems to think
the same. His head snaps over his shoulder, but she's
nowhere to be seen. There is loud swearing from the

kitchen and something smashes. Merc's eyes flick up to meet mine. They're wary: "did you tell her?"

"Mum? No way, man! She's just being mum – wants to check you okay."

His eyes are ice, scanning me.

Then: "okay."

He checks his pocket for his keys and pulls the door closed. He has nothing on his feet and his white hair is all over the place.

"You look like Einstein," I manage.

He grins. That blinding grin like someone opening a cage door.

"…but you smell like shit."

By the time we make it to my front door, he has me in a headlock, my nose firmly in his super-stinky armpit.

I think it's going to be ok, especially when Mum wrinkles her nose and points at the bathroom – and he goes.

<u>Mercutio</u>

So, here I am, back at school. What else am I going to do? I suppose I could just stop. Go away or something. Nobody would bother to find me. It makes me want to laugh just thinking about Aggie discovering I was missing. I imagine her shrugging and going through my stuff for loose change.

"Mark!" Miss Brown has her beady eyes firmly on me, like she's expecting something. Her pen is poised over the whiteboard. They all call me Mark – I think someone must have written it down somewhere. If I went missing they would all be looking for a Mark…

"The peasants," Miss Brown insists, "why did they revolt?"

I haven't a clue.

"Sorry, Miss," I say, "I can't concentrate - I've got such a bad headache."

I rub my eyes for effect and squint in her general direction. Behind me, Romeo sniggers just loud enough for me to hear. Miss Brown pauses – to pursue or not to pursue. She decides not to.

"Go get a drink of water," she says.

"Thanks, Miss."

I catch Romeo's smirk as I head for the door. Too bad – he'll have to do the rest of whatever this is, without my participation.

It's good to be out in the empty corridors, my footsteps echoing like I'm a sole survivor. I decide to take the long way. There's at least 40 minutes left of the period, so I have at least 30 minutes to burn. I head to the water fountain at the furthest end of building. Not that I'm thirsty or anything, but it's good to look like I'm doing what I said I would.

Everyone is in lessons. There is a rote language learning somewhere and I can hear the hum of voices repeating phrases over and over. Like monks saying penance.

I hang around the water fountain a bit, but it's a boring part of the school and there's nothing to see. I'm wondering what to do next when I find half a fag at the bottom of my pocket. Raj keeps a lighter in the bicycle shed, so I head out there.

It's not really a bicycle shed. It's just what they call it now because they have bicycle racks in it. It used to just be a store shed. They've opened up the front a bit for the bicycle racks, but it's still deep and there are places at the back where you can be out of sight long enough for a quick smoke.

It's just starting to rain when I head out across the field and its proper pelting it down as I get into the shed. I'm proper wet and the rain running from my hair down my collar gets at my shirt under the blazer. My shoes are sloshing so much that I have to take them off and empty them out. Not that I care. It's not cold and it's a bit of fun. I even laugh to myself, like a proper nutter.

Raj's lighter is on the high beam at the back and, after giving it a good shake, I light up. I don't smoke a lot, but this one tastes good. I feel like someone from a TV advert with the rain hammering the tin above my head and school almost disappeared across the field. Like I'm the invisible man.

"Fancy meeting you here."

He makes me jump and I almost drop my fag.

Dion.

He's standing perfectly still in the corner, with his blazer collar turned up to his neck so that his shirt doesn't show. He pulls on his fag and the end lights up like a little caution beacon.

I say nothing, just wait. My cigarette end is burning out between my fingers. I take a quick puff and drop the butt to the floor. I gotta go, but I don't know how to make it look right.

Somehow, Dion has moved closer.

"I heard all about Cheryl," he says. His voice is flat, neutral. I don't know why he would say that.

"She likes to get what she wants." I don't know why he would say that either.

"Reckon you might have upset her…" He is just talking to himself.

I don't look at him, just move to go. But then his hand is on the back of my neck.

Shit.

I wait to see what he will do next. I'm ready. My hands are out of my pockets. Ready, but I try to keep the tension out of my neck, so he doesn't know it too.

"Yeah," I say. I try to sound casual, like I'm not in a bicycle shed with a bloke who is going to hit me. What else can I say? I don't turn around, but I feel him standing very close behind me. So close, I can feel his breath on the edge of my ear- hot and quick. I wait for him to hit me.

But he doesn't. He just stands there and breathes, like he doesn't know what to do next.

I shrug his hand off my neck. I should just walk away, but I turn around. He's just standing there, looking at me - like he's stuck. We're so close that I can see there are tiny beads of sweat on his upper lip.

"Hey, you okay, mate?" In the moment, I mean it.

But he just looks at me, his eyes flickering over my face like he wants to say something. Not dangerous, just weird.

He's really looking at me and his mouth opens and closes likes he's trying to catch at words.

"Hey, Dion – you okay?"

His arm moves and I think he's going to hit me, but he just sort-of reaches for my face. I duck out of the way.

"What the hell?!"

That snaps him out of it and he slaps me hard across the ear.

"Fuck off, Mark. This is my shed."

He doesn't have to ask twice, but I don't run. I walk through the rain so that I am dripping by the time I arrive back at the building.

Just for a moment, I look to see if Dion is headed back too, but the bike shed is just a dark hump on the other side of the field.

Something strange flutters in my chest. Something trying to get out. A weird sort of homing beacon that I can't quite see. I try to catch it, but it's gone, just out of reach.

<u>Dion</u>

Dunno what it is about that kid. Feels like I've been watching him forever. I don't aim to – he's just always there. That white hair that stands out like some sort of flag. I dunno. It calls to me. Makes me sick. And the Cheryl story is doing my head in. Dunno why.

I'm proper snuck into the corner when I see someone coming. I know I'm invisible, I've been here before, but I turn up the collar of my blazer so that my shirt doesn't show, just in case. I'll put out the fag if it's a teacher.

But its him. The water is running off him in streams so that his skin looks polished, like that white stone in sculptures. Marble. Like someone has sculpted him out of marble – all hard and liquid at once. His hair is plastered down and as he pushes it out of his eyes, water flicks like spit. He doesn't see me.

I watch him when he reaches for the top beam. Everyone knows there's a lighter there – bloody miracle it still has some juice.

The wet shirt sticks as he reaches up. I can see his ribs and the hard line of his side to where his hip bone is. Somewhere, something inside catches and suddenly I can't breathe. I dunno why.

I just watch for a bit. He thinks he is all alone and his face relaxes. He almost smiles.

Then I talk.

He says nothing, but I can see his back straighten. He thinks I'm going to hit him. I sort-of want to, but when I get close to him, it's just weird. Just weird.

I feel like I've been waiting for years. Just waiting. I dunno what for. Waiting for something.

When I hit him, I want to grab hold of him too, but I push him out into the rain and he goes.

The moment he's gone, I know I've messed up. I can't seem to remember the details, but I know … I just know.

What if he runs off and tells his mates? What if Kev hears? What did I do?

I sit in the corner of the shed. The rain is smashing into the steel roof and I can't even see the school anymore.

There's a bitter ball of worry in my chest and I'm so cold that my legs are starting to cramp.

I'll kill him if he says one single word.

"I'll kill him."

But even though I say the words out loud, all I can think about is the water running off his skin. His skin, like marble.

<u>Mercutio</u>

It's gone midnight before Aggie and Roger or Dodger or Slodger - whoever - finally stop giggling and go to sleep. I can stop watching the door and watch the sky instead.

Something is blinking in the dark. Satellite or star, I dunno. Just something out there bright enough to still shine above the city.

I haven't really thought about what happened. I don't really know what happened there in the bike shed with Dion.

I slip into sleep and the wet smell of the shed is in my nostrils. The rain hammers against the corrugated iron of the roof like a heartbeat. A hand curls around my neck, the thumb behind my ear. Someone is breathing warm against my shoulder and I know, without looking, the hands, the face behind me. I know that breath, the certain friendship of that hand.

More.

Romeo.

I blink awake in the dark.

A warm longing is curled tightly in my belly. I am crying, but I don't know why.

***

The phone pings. Like water dripping in a basin when everything else is quiet. Tiny and turbulent.

He is afraid to look, but a tap on the screen flashes the words : `Out of theatre. All good.'

And now he can't stop reading. Just five words. He reads then again and again, looking for clues. Nothing. All good.

But nothing to fill up the gap in his heart. All good.

He is holding the phone so hard that his hand is beginning to cramp, the fingers, with the nail edges still dark with blood, clamped like claws. All good.

He is surprised that he is shaking. The tremors pulse through him with such violence that he has to lie down and wait for it to pass like a fit.

He doesn't cry. Not now.

All good.

BEFORE

<u>Romeo</u>

Mum always says; " the more things change, the more they stay the same."

Now me, I'm not so sure I agree. Things change all the time. It feels like things are changing now. I mean, here we are, the end of school in sight and all our futures laid out there. It's flippin' huge and scary and well, just, normal too. This growing up and moving on story. I reckon I'm ready.

Ready to be an adult and all that stuff. Take on a career, y'know. Maybe pay Mum back for some of the stuff she's done for me.

Mum wants Uni for me. Reckon I do too. Sixth form first – want to take Maths. Yeah, right? Merc just about fainted when I told him. Dunno what Merc has planned. He doesn't talk about it. Reckon moving on scares him a bit – he's not exactly the social type and I don't reckon he thinks about us all going away from each other.

I've been going to extra Maths with Ben; looking for that top grade y'know. Merc tried coming too, but classrooms aren't really his thing – especially not extra classrooms. I think he hates that me and Ben are doing something he doesn't want to do, but hey, I gotta do something for me. Merc is my mate – the best mate a guy could have – but I can't be worrying about him all the time. But I do. Merc: all hard and cold, like frozen metal that will just shatter if you hit it the wrong way.

I feel bad, but this is life – we gotta grow up.

Then there's Tannita. I couldn't breathe when I saw her in the back of the class. I didn't know a girl could be so beautiful. So perfect. I know how mad that sounds, but the moment I saw her, I knew she was perfect.

So I go to Maths to see Tannita too. Talk to her, maybe.

I wait for her when the class ends.

"Hi."

She looks at me like she has only just seen me. Her eyes are dark and wide and soft, like Bambi's eyes.

"Hi."

I can see Ben grinning at me without looking.

"Can I walk with you?" I ask. It sounds stupid, not cool at all, but I can't think of anything else to say.

Her mouth smiles and her teeth are white and perfect.

"Okay," she says. So I walk with her. Just me and her. It feels like walking a new path. Like a new beginning.

<u>Dion</u>

Nothing happens. Dad is reading some article about some celebrity. He grunts and mutters as he reads, his forehead in a permanent frown. I watch him from over my cup. He hasn't changed much, on the outside at least. Just less hair and more wrinkles. It's the inside that has changed. It's like he has gotten smaller and smaller on the inside with less and less room for any good news.

I'm glad I'm different to him.

I look at my hands. The palms are hard from the labouring job that keeps me from going mental between college days. Weird, but there's something soothing about swinging a sledgehammer and picking up rubble, feeling the strength of your own body. Being useful.

Dad got me the job – some contact. "It's all about contacts," he says.

He shakes the paper. Who still reads a paper? Who still walks to the corner shop and buys a paper?

"Bunch of no-good deviants," he mutters. His nose does that quick wrinkled sniff of disapproval. The headlines are full of youth violence. Knife crime is a big thing, apparently. Some other kid has been stabbed to death just outside his school. I wonder what would make you do it …

Gran pricks up her ears: "What now?"

Dad hurrumphs on about "the kids today – no discipline…" and then he slides into some ramble about "stupid celebrities saying stupid things and why don't they just wear normal clothes…"

Gran goes off at a tangent: "I think it's just the fashion, all these people so confused now. When I was a girl, women were women and men were men. And we had respect. It was all proper. None of this rubbish about kids going around killing each other…"

I want to remind her about the Krays, but I don't think they were kids, so I shut up.

She is on a roll though: "And why is everybody gay now? We never knew gay people when I was young…"

I want to tell her that's because they were all in hiding, but I may as well talk to a wall. Dad and Gran are cut from the same cloth and long exposure to the vacuum of each other has made their minds ever smaller.

"It's just not natural…" Gran finishes with a sigh, her disappointment with the world clear as she goes back to doing her crossword.

In the vacuum of silence that follows her outburst, an image of white hair suddenly flashes into my mind, the sinews of his neck tight under my hand, his pulse beating in my fingertips. The feeling of being within reach of home.

It's been almost a year, but there's still a clamp that grabs at my throat; a yearning that reaches for me from the place I have tucked it away - somewhere dark and deep. And the feeling of shame and loss that follows close behind.

I battle to push the memory aside, but a warm blush is creeping up my neck and I look to see if they see. Dad has his face in the paper and Gran is counting letters.

"Gotta go," I manage.

Dad mutters something and I go, shutting the door to that crappy little flat with its smell of cabbage (why is that? We never even eat cabbage!). Years. Dad always said it would be temporary - `just while things settle' – and here we are, still living with Gran. There was always something, some reason why we couldn't go. First it was that I needed watching and then that rentals were too steep and the latest is that Gran needs the company. Whatever. I stopped dreaming about moving out a long time ago, but I'm an adult now, mostly, so soon I'll be making my own plans.

Kev tells me there's a business opportunity. Won't say what, but he reckons it looks like a way to earn a steady income. I told him I won't do illegal stuff, but he reckons it's all upfront. Not long now and I'll be able to move on, be my own man.

Dad still thinks Kev's bad news, but he's still the only one giving me a break. A real break I mean, not a minimum wage job and the slow grinding of this college qualification. It's like time is stuck.

I wonder if life happened in High School and all I am doing now if waiting. Waiting for something to happen. Maybe it's time to make it happen.

Outside, it's bright – a perfect early Summer's day. It's good to be out of stuffiness of the flat and away from Dad and Gran. It feels good to have something happening at last. I push the image of the white-haired boy deep back into my memory. That was then and this is now – onwards and upwards!

Kev is waiting on the usual corner. He hasn't changed a bit. Got a kid now – Seany – but he lives with his mum. Kev says it's good to be a dad and that Seany is the best thing that's happened to him.

"But it's tough keeping the reddies rolling in – responsibility and all," he says.

Not me. I don't want a family – they're just full of shit. Weigh you down. Don't have to look far to see the truth of that. I just want to make some money and to get out of here.

`Hey, my man!' We bump fists. He still looks exactly the same – not like a dad at all.

"So, what's happ'nin?"

"Waiting on a deal," says Kev. He's watching the street. His mate, Ronan is watching too. They seem on edge. My heart sinks a bit.

"Yeah? What deal?"

"Wait and see, Boy-oh, wait and see." He cuffs me gently on the ear. He is acting all smooth, but I can see his leg shaking like it does when he's nervous. He gets up off the wall when he sees a group coming.

There's six of them and they bowl along down the pavement towards us, all swagger. The one in the front is tall and skinny, sort of like he's in a teenage time-warp. The scar has gotten whiter with age.

Tim Ashby.

"What the hell, Kev?"

"Shuddup. Its business."

Him and Ronan go to greet Tim. There's handshakes and first bumps and they light a fag to share. Tim Ashby nods at me. I nod back, but that anticipation has turned to apprehension and is crawling along my spine like ants.

I'm not an idiot, though Dad would tell you I am, I know what Kev's deal is: small time fencing – wing mirrors and hub caps, a bit of copper wire, stuff that sometimes falls off trucks. Enough to make a buck but not attract too much attention. Never been in jail, Kevin, not even been stopped by the cops. Reckon maybe he's not quite the idiot dad thinks he is, either.

 But I'm not sure about this plan. Tim Ashby is into bad shit. Must be, because the rumour is that he's making thousands. I want nothing to do with him. Every instinct is telling me to walk away, but Kev's blood, so I stay.

I can see Tim's mate eying me. He says something and Kev waves me over.

"Hey, Dion, you know Tim?" He waves us in the direction of each other.

"Sure," I say and lean in to bump Tim's fist. I'm surprised to find that he is shorter than me and the fist that bumps mine is bony, the knuckles like marbles.

He doesn't bother to look at me.

"Cool," he says.

To Kev he says: "so a try out and then we'll see."

Kev nods.

"Cool," says Tim and he walks away, his posse closing around him. One of them takes a blade out of his pocket. Its one of those that flicks in and out. He flicks it as he walks, the little snap of the blade marking time as they leave. It feels like a threat.

Kev and Ronan grin at each other.

"C'mon Kev, " I say, "not Tim Ashby…"

But Kev has pound signs in his eyes and he thumps me, before grabbing me in a headlock.

"Chill, " he says before letting go , "it's all good. No stress, bruv!"

I grin because Kev is my mate, but the bad feeling is in the back of my throat, like a lump I can't swallow. Tim Ashby isn't known for his loyalty. Anything to do with Tim Ashby is going to end badly.

<u>Mercutio</u>

It's a bit like heaven – here in the sun on Bettina's sofa on a Saturday morning, us all together. Me and Rom do separate stuff now. Studies and stuff. Bettina keeps saying he's gotta `buckle down' if he's going to get into a good school. She says I should too, but I reckon my prospects are limited, so why waste my time listening to some teacher droning on? Doesn't matter. Reckon Romeo will do good for both of us.

The flat is full of the sweet smell of pancakes and Bettina is humming along to the radio. I watch her as she jigs and flips, the pancakes growing in a stack like a wonky tree stump. Romeo is chilled on the other side of the sofa, his faced turned into the sun so that his skin shines. His eyes are closed and he is grinning to himself, one finger tapping to the music. He is so beautiful. Sounds stupid to say about a boy, but he is.

I want to say aloud that this is where I want to be forever. Here, in the sun with Romeo. I want to be able to stretch out my hand and touch him. I wish I was brave.

Instead, I close my eyes and pretend that we are just brothers, hanging in the sun and that Bettina is our mum and she loves us both.

"Nearly done," Bettina says, "lots of energy for the two of you to get studying done, nah?"

I glance at Bettina and she catches my eye and flicks her head in Romeo's direction.

"Look at loverboy," she says with a grin and rolls her eyes.

For a moment, I think she knows and my heart jumps, but she is laughing.

"Thinking about Tannita?" She asks loudly. She draws out the syllables so that they become long and musical : Taa -nee- ta.

Romeo's eyes flick open and he grins. There is something shy in the way he looks at us.

"Ma-aa…"

Tannita? My heart pounds. A sour lump of betrayal is clogging my throat.

"Tannita?" I manage.

"Yeah, man, you know…"

I don't know.

"Lily's friend – the girl with the hair…" his hands move through the air as if he is sketching her. His face is lit up. "Tannita."

I try to remember who she is, but I feel sick. Suddenly I am cold and the smell of pancakes makes me want to puke. How come I don't know?

Bettina has a hand on my head: "You okay, Sweetie? You don't look so good.''

I stutter that I don't feel well. I can't meet their eyes as I make for the door.

Tannita.

Someone he found without me.

Tannita. And Romeo's shy smile at the sound of her name.

Loverboy.

For Tannita.

Without me.

"Hey Merc?" Romeo is running down the stairs behind me.

His hand is on my shoulder and I try to shrug it off, but my shoulder just jumps a bit under his hand.

"Hey Merc," he says and I stop and wait for him to say something. Anything.

"Sorry, Mate," he says, "I thought you knew. Y'know, when me and Ben go to revision. I met her there. I think you know her…"

Bloody Ben. It was always going to be him.

"Nah," I try to sound casual, but my voice cracks and I have to clear my throat. I can't bring myself to look at him. "Nope. No. You didn't tell me."

The words sound pathetic when they come out. Pathetic and inadequate, like some little kid trying to say something that there are no words for. I want to say : "you lied to me! You made me love you and now you lied to me!" But I can't, so I stand there and don't look at him.

"Merc," his voice is warm, "Merc, this changes nothing, bruv. Nothing. You're still my best mate. Nothing will ever change that."

I nod, but it's a lie. This changes everything. Every dream. Us. Things are already changed. Tannita. Best mate isn't enough.

"C'mon, Merc. We're brothers, you and me," he puts his arms around my shoulders and then hugs me. For just a moment I am overwhelmed by the smell and feel of him. How warm he is. He smells of pancakes and sunshine and something else that is just Romeo.

I don't hug him back, but my head nods like I'm an idiot.

"C'mon, Merc," he says, "c'mon – all those pancakes to be eaten..."

He is grinning at me and I am forced to grin back so that he cuffs me around the ear and starts back up the stairs. All I can do is follow. He is my best mate, my brother. I hate him and love him all at once. And I can't be without him, so I go.

"So, what's this Tannita like?" I try to keep my voice neutral, to not sound mocking.

His face lights up like I've flipped a switch. "Gorgeous, man," he says, "just gorgeous."

His eyes look at her though me. He doesn't see me at all.

When we get back to the flat, the pancakes are in the centre of the little table with a bowl of cinnamon sugar and a bottle of lemon juice.

"Hurry up, boys," Bettina calls cheerily from the sink, "they're getting cold..."

I feel her eyes on me and when I look, her gaze looks into me. I try to smile it away but it feels stiff and false.

Romeo gets stuck in and I sit down opposite him.

The day is still beautiful, the sun is still streaming in through the window. The flat still smells of warmth and pancakes. Romeo gabbles on and Bettina adds details, like they are trying to reassure me.

Her name is Tannita and she's what Bettina calls ` a good girl'. I suppose she must be – because Romeo chose her. Nothing like Cheryl or Aggie. Maybe a bit like Bettina.

And like that, just like that, everything changes. For a minute, while Romeo and Bettina are in their own thoughts, I look at him: let my eyes travel across his broad forehead and along the high bone of his cheek, goldened in the sun, to where it drops softly to that full and smiling mouth. The hollow of his throat, where his heart pulses. Where my heart pulses until I look away.

I wonder if he knows. It doesn't matter. Even if he does know, he's made a choice. You can't love a best mate that way any-way. Not even a brother. My heart twists.

Romeo's eyes flick across to me and he grins a hamster grin, his cheeks full of pancake: "Excellent!"

Maybe this is all the happy there can be. Here, now, in this little council flat with the sun pouring in the window.

"Excellent," I say and I find that I can smile, for real - because he is smiling and I still love him.

Bettina smiles softly at us both and when she reaches for a pancake, her hand closes over mine for just a moment. She squeezes my fingers softly.

"So," she says lightly while rolling a pancake, "what you boys up to, huh?"

Romeo shrugs, his mouth full.

"Just hangin' out," he says at last, " Merc?"

He grins and I sort-of nod. Yeah, just hanging out.

"Tannita will be there," Romeo says, his eyes flicking quickly over mine. He downplays it: "at some point. Ben and Lily too. Just hanging out…"

And there I will be. There, but not there, because … because they found each other without me. There they will be in their postcard couples and I will be alone again.

It's like Bettina hears me.

"You'll have to find yourself a nice girl, Mercutio," she says softly and kisses my head, her arms held wide so that she doesn't drop anything sticky on me.

I nod, but I don't look at Romeo. I just concentrate on eating pancakes and getting back to that nice feeling of being warm and safe.

Aggie is always saying that nothing good lasts forever. She is right, but I can't understand why not.

<u>Dion</u>

"It's just a trial," he keeps saying, but the bad feeling grows and grows as we walk.

The details are sketchy. I know that anything to do with Tim Ashby is a bad plan, but Kev says it'll be simple.

"It's just moving stuff. We pick it up, we drop it off… C'mon bruv – you agreed…"

He is getting irritated with me and his jaw has gotten tight.

"Yeah, I know, but I don't think it's right. What is the stuff?" I demand. I think I have a pretty good idea what it is, but I'm not going to say it outright.

"No clue." Says Kev with conviction. "We don't ask, we don't look, we just do."

"Why aren't Tim's boys doing it?"

"Ah come on, Dion!" He throws his hands in the air. "It doesn't matter. This is a chance, bruv. We do good here and there's a chance to get some prospects. A chance for some proper cash. Just once is all it takes, bruv."

"Yeah," I think, "just once to get caught."

I know why Tim Ashby's boys aren't doing it – it's not their turf. We're going to be out there taking all the risks because the local gangs don't know us.

"We need you…" Kev's tone has changed and his arm is over my shoulder like when I was a lost little kid and needed him. I owe him. I owe him a lot.

I know it's a bad plan. I know we should stay a million miles away. But its Kev, so I crumble. Again.

"Okay," I nod, "but its 'cos you asked me, not for the money and not for Tim Ashby."

He grabs my head between both hands and puts his forehead against mine, like he used to.

"That's my man!"

He is grinning now and the tension disappears like mist into the perfect day. We sit on the wall and share a smoke.

Just once. Some guys do this all the time. Maybe it'll be okay.

The doubt gnaws away at my gut. Just once.

* * *

Breathe.

He doesn't know how long he has been asleep, curled tight against the edge of the bed.

Not long – the morning is just creeping into the sky and the city hasn't yet begun to buzz.

Somewhere in the building he can hear a baby crying and he sits up.

Breathe.

Now.

It is now.

AFTER

<u>Romeo</u>

This is how Saturdays should be: the long afternoon just goes on and on, spilling into the evening that feels slow like dripping syrup. There's not even a breeze and we get so hot sitting in this crappy little park that we have to go and find a tree to sit under. Doesn't matter where we sit, to be honest. Tannita's hand is in mine; I can feel her pulse jumping straight from her fingers to my heart. She's giggling at something that Lily said and it's like a river – just washes everything away so that all I can hear is her.

She's proper beautiful. I never thought that anyone could be so beautiful. Not like those movie stars and their pumped-up lips and pouty photos. Nothing like that. She just looks, I dunno – perfect. Little, but round in the right places and her eyes are dark like wood and leaves and being warm. And her hair! Man, her hair! It's this cloud that is all around her head like some sort of shiny black halo. Proper beautiful.

We're hangin' in the square near the play park. It's not exactly picturesque, but we've got a piece of grass and the tree still has some blossom that keeps falling down and sticking in Tannita's hair like confetti.

Lily keeps picking it out: "looks like you're getting bloody married," she laughs and Tannita looks at me.

We're just hangin, waiting for it to get late enough to get some food. Merc was here for a bit. He sat away from us – not away, away, just a bit apart. I think maybe him and Tannita don't know what to do with each other. When Merc is around, Tannita stands close to me like she's a bit scared and Merc stands a bit away like he's scared too. Weird. Merc isn't scared of anything, dunno why a tiny thing like Tannita makes him so jumpy.

"I reckon Merc misses you," Ben says suddenly while the girls are nattering. He has his eyes closed against the sun and he talks like he is half asleep.

"Yeah?" I know Ben is right, but what can I do?

Mum says this is part of growing up : "you have to get on with things," she says, `life is about moving forward."

"Yeah." I say.

"Maybe the girls can hook him up?" Ben says doubtfully and he opens his eyes to watch Tannita and Lilly as they talk. I know we are both remembering the Cheryl incident.

"Maybe…"

Lily starts laughing: "Mark? You talking about finding Mark a girlfriend?"

She laughs so hard that she snorts. I dunno what she finds so funny.

Then she says: "he's too much of a weirdo!"

I think of Merc and his long spider fingers, those eyes that are ice and warm at once. The way that he smiles – like a door opening onto something wonderful.

"That's not kind…" says Tannita. She looks at me like I should be saying something. Her voice is soft like honey and her hand creeps into mine.

"Nope," I say, too late, "and its wrong. Merc is one of the best guys you could know."

Lily snorts again. "Doesn't matter how you say it, there's no way I'd go with Mark!"

She flicks her hair and leans into Ben, but Ben won't have it and pushes her off. He is frowning, angry in a way I don't understand.

"You're outta line," he says stiffly and Lily gets all cross and pouty.

"You're being mean," she says.

"Just honest," says Ben and he's right, but Lily is weighing things up in that weird way that girls do – and she's not happy.

"Fine…" she says, getting to her feet and wiping the grass off her backside. "Fine. You keep your weird friend, Ben. And you, Romeo. The whole world knows that Mark only has eyes for you…"

"Oi!" says Ben, but Lily throws him the goose and flounces off, her hair swinging like the butt of an agitated horse.

Tannita makes to go after her, but I pull her back.

"Nah," says Ben, all cool and easy again, "let her go – she's an idiot." He pats my shoulder. "We know Merc and there's nothing weird about him. Okay – a bit weird, but good weird…"

We grin at each other. Yup. We know Merc. I know he's the best friend I ever had.

I think of the way he fought for me when I was a little kid. How he always used to play whatever game I wanted to. Then I think of his mum standing in the doorway of their flat, of the paint peeling in the hall. Of the smell of damp. I think about when we met – how he was so skinny. It's like a bright light suddenly flips on in my head and I feel stupid and guilty.

"Yup," I say, "he's the best friend anyone could have." And I mean it, because suddenly I know why Mum has looked at him like that for all these years – and why I'm a crap friend.

We see Merc coming back from wherever he went - that long loping walk and the shock of white hair that stands up no matter what. Even though he is too far away to see, I know that he will be looking at me - those ice eyes missing nothing.

"The best friend," I say again, but I'm saying it for me.

<u>Mercutio</u>

She's wide-eyed and wild-haired. She talks with a foreign accent and her slim little hands tuck like gloves into Romeo's. He looks at her like she is a miracle and something in her lights up when she looks back at him.

When she looks at me, her eyes stumble, like she doesn't know what to do. But I guess she's okay because Romeo is happy. I can't hate her because he is happy.

I know I should leave them alone, not hang around like some sort of lost fart, but I can't. If I'm not with Rom, where else can I be?

So I come back to them where they have been all day without me. I feel like some sort of animal: like I have to go back to the herd, even though I know I don't fit. It's like I don't know what I am if I'm not with them.

Him.

So I come back to where they are sitting in the last of the sun. The light makes Romeo shine. Tannita too.

We hang around until it's starting to get dark, talking crap. Ben is looking at me and not looking, like he wants to say something. I dunno what happened while I was gone, but Lily has gone off somewhere. I don't ask. She's more of the same and I don't know why Ben bothers.

Something has changed in Tannita. She smiles at me suddenly and she smiles with her eyes, like something good has passed between us. I like her enough. It's just Rom. The way he smiles into her causes a jolt of pain in the middle of my chest. But it's okay. If he's okay, I'm okay. What else can I be?

"I'm staaarving," says Ben at last, stretching his arms above his head and yawning. I want to tell him that he's not – that he has never been starving, but I don't say anything.

"Chippie?" he suggests.

I don't have any money, but I nod any-way.

"Yup," says Rom and he hauls Tannita to her feet.

We walk together, Tannita and Rom in the middle and me and Ben on the sides. It's a slow, warm evening and the streetlights are just starting to come on. It's nice – relaxed. Even the traffic is chilled and the cars that pass us seem to purr like friendly cats. Ben is humming some familiar tune and I find that, after a while, I don't even mind that Romeo keeps whispering things in Tannita's ear.

Our local chippie isn't far – just two streets down, but there's a bunch of kids waiting outside. They're having some sort of party and they are singing loudly. I feel a bit sick when I see that Cheryl is front and centre, arm in arm with Lily. They are belting out some song that twangs like tin from a phone in the background. They are having too much fun to see us. Romeo stops. He looks at me.

"Not this chippie," he says.

"'S okay…" I start to say, but Romeo grins at me : "Tannita fancies something else." She nods, agrees, meets my eyes and smiles.

"Something different," she agrees. "A bit of a walk, but it'll be worth it…"

I can see that Ben wants to say something and I want him to. To say that this is all stupid.

I could just go home. Leave this. I want to, but I can't.

Tannita and Romeo turn and walk in the opposite direction. Ben looks at the girls dancing and singing and then back at me. I know he wants to hang out with them, but then there I am, a gooseberry if he doesn't come along, so he shrugs and we follow. I feel stupid. Like the object of pity. Its good when we turn the corner and can't hear the stupid out-of-tune singing any more.

<u>Dion</u>

So far, so easy.

All I have to do is walk a bit behind Kev and Ronan and check that nobody's clocked us. Easy. Not that my heart isn't trying to climb out of my mouth.

"Easy, fella," Kev said when we started out, "no matter what goes down, you're not involved, innit? You just keep a watch, is all."

It is kinda easy. We hang around a bus stop for a while until the number 145 comes in, then I go on hedge inspection while Kev and Ronan meet with some bloke and his backpack. It's getting dark, but not so much that I can't see what's happening. The bloke nods at Kev. Kev nods back and swings the backpack over his shoulder.

Now it is just a case of walking.

I follow at a distance as Kev and Ronan head for where they are supposed to meet Ashby. It's a shit part of town. Just the other side of a high street and there are locked up buildings covered with graffiti – like the sort of thing you'd see in a gangster movie. I amuse myself by pretending that I'm an undercover cop following two perps, but Kev looks back and laughs at me as I pretend-duck behind a pillar, so I go back to just walking. I hang back a bit so that it doesn't look obvious that I am with them and I slow right down when Kev flicks his cigarette butt into the street. That's the signal.

He turns the corner and is gone from sight until I get to the edge of the brick building and peek round. It's a sort of alley-way, dark between the two warehouses, darker than it should be at this time. There is just a single light halfway down. Kev and Ronan are two shadows moving away from me, but I can see Tim Ashby clearly in the light. It does him no favours – even from where I am I can see his scar lit up like a snail trail across his face. There are three or four guys with him, but they're more in the dark and I can't make out who they are.

My gut twists. Something feels off. Even more off than meeting a petty criminal in a dark side-street…

I watch Kev moving into the light. He fist-bumps Tim and hands over the backpack. Tim doesn't even look at it – he hands it straight over his shoulder to some bloke behind. A minute later and that bloke's hair blinks in the light as he says something in Tim's ear.

Tim nods. He fist-bumps at Kev and turns to go.

"Oi!" I hear Kev say, loud into the echo of the alleyway.

Tim turns around. Slow. He looks at Kev. His shoulders are slightly hunched over – the look of someone ready to fight.

I can see Kev more now that he has moved into the light. His hands are out and his head is pushed forward. I know he is asking about being paid.

Tim looks at him and I see his mouth moving, but I can't hear what he says. He turns away and Kev grabs him by the shoulder.

Shit! I start to run without thinking.

The group under the light has closed in, Tim's boys' heads glinting. They don't seem to make a sound.

Away, at the other side of the alley, I think I see people moving, but they're just shapes.

"Kev!" I call as I run, "leave it!" My voice is loud against the walls.

But it's too late. Kev has hit Tim and all hell has broken loose.

"Hey!" someone is shouting and running from the far end of the alleyway, their shoes slapping echoes in the narrow space. I don't know if it was me who shouted.

"Hey!" I just want to stop Kev from being killed.

<u>Mercutio</u>

I dunno where we're headed – it's a place Tannita knows.

"It'll be good," Romeo grins at me through her cloud of hair. We turn off the High Street and head towards the station, taking the backways. "This way is quicker," Rom says.

It's quieter here. Offices and shut shops.

When we've gone a little way, Ben pulls on my elbow and winks at me. We drop back from the other two, letting them walk on ahead, their heads close together. They don't seem to notice where we are.

It's pathetic, but the slower I walk, the more I feel like Rom is pulling away from me – moving into another place that I can't reach. I want to pull him back, but I say nothing. Just slow down and walk with Ben, watching as the gap between me and my friend gets bigger and bigger. I wish I hadn't come. I wish I had just gone for a walk by myself. Pathetic.

"Down here! Not far now…" Tannita calls out, her face turning briefly back to us, like a coin in the streetlights. She and Rom turn into an alleyway between two buildings.

I hate alleyways.

"I hope we get there soon, I'm flippin' starving!" grumbles Ben.

I'm about to say I've had enough too, when the whole world shifts. Suddenly there is yelling coming from the dark space ahead and Rom's voice calls clearly: "Hey! Watch out!"

Then Tannita is screaming and screaming and screaming.

It's just an instant and we are running, turning into the alleyway where the sudden darkness blinds us and I can't make sense of what I see. A single weak light breaks the dark and there are shadows of people running away like finger puppets against a wall. The beat of their feet slams against the closeness of the alley. My blood is rushing in my ears and I can't tell if its two or twenty, but I'm sure I see the silver glint of a blade before it disappears. My brain is stupid and slow and I can't understand. Where is Rom?

There is dark heap on the ground under the lamp and Tannita is folded over it and screaming. Then I see – Romeo.

`Fuck,' says Ben. He pulls Tannita away and rolls Romeo over.

I just stand.

Rom's white T-shirt has a dark splodge that is growing out from his chest, like a great big poppy is blooming over his heart.

`Fuck,' says Ben. Tannita has stopped screaming and is crying in long gulps.

Then Romeo opens his eyes and looks at me. Those eyes that hold everything.

"Merc?" his mouth says. I am down on my knees. My hand is pressing hard against the place where the blood is pumping out like oil. My other hand is glued to his.

"Don't die, don't die, don't die," I say over and over and over, but the words don't come out. I press my hand on his chest and try to press my heartbeat into him. "Don't die."

Dimly I hear Ben talking to the emergency services.

It is forever before they come and prize my fingers away from him.

"Let go, son, it's okay, let go." But my hand is welded: "don't die."

He is still conscious. "Good" they say. They rig him up to a drip, there in the alleyway that smells of piss.

And he says one word : "Tannita."

She is crying and shaking, but she walks with him to the ambulance. Climbs inside. Sits with him when they close the door.

My heart is so numb that it takes long minutes to break.

The police are here, but I can't hear them. Ben is talking and talking and one of them keeps saying something to me, but I can't make sense of it.

"Bettina." My mouth says and Ben talks some more. "Bettina." My mouth says again.

One of the police officers has found a cup of tea and puts it into my hand. It sticks to the blood. There is one of those foil blankets around my shoulders. I dunno how it got there.

One of the officers tries to walk with me, but my legs won't work.

It's like they are talking from far away. "Take you home…" I hear but it makes no sense. Why would I want to go home? My body won't move.

"C'mon son," the policeman is trying to push me and my mouth won't work to say "no." My body feels like lead.

Then Ben is there. "It's okay," he says, "I'll get him home."

So they go and Ben stands there with me under the streetlight. Rom's blood is everywhere. It blinks back the glow of the streetlight in miniature, like light falling down a well.

Ben is rubbing my shoulder. It's a stupid thing to do, but it's good to have him here.

"C'mon, Merc," he says, "time to go."

Where? Where will I go when Romeo isn't there?

"C'mon, mate," he says.

Then it's just there. Like my mind has come unstuck – like a sudden spotlight – the picture of Dion in my mind. His face looking back. Holding someone else, someone hunched over. Just a split second – his eyes looking back and seeing me. Dion.

The sudden knowledge is like an electric shock.

I start walking and Ben has to jog to keep up.

<u>Dion</u>

I knew it! I knew Tim Ashby couldn't be trusted and I know it again as I start to run. I am shouting at Kev, but it's too late – he's hit Tim in the face and Tim and his boys are bent forward, fists flailing.

I think I'm only a metre or so away when I see the blade. It's a flash in the streetlight. Silver and sudden, but it repeats like a strobe. Flash, flash, flash between Tim and Kev and Kev is doubled over by the time I get to him.

Then someone comes barrelling through Ashby's boys from behind and takes Tim down, dark skin in the dark. I see Ashby roll and the blade like a fish in the light. A girl is screaming, but I don't stop to look. Kev is stumbling and I wrap my arm around his body, hitching his shoulder onto mine. Somehow Ronan has got his other side and we pull and drag him away. He's making gasping noises and his weight slumps heavy.

"C'mon, Kev, walk!"

There's shouting from the other end of the alleyway and the slap of running feet. Fear grabs at my throat, but when I look back all I can see is that someone is down under the streetlight. That girl is screaming and screaming and then he's there – the hair like a banner coming in from the dark.

My stomach jerks and I turn and move as fast as I can, Kev's feet stumbling to keep up.

<u>Mercutio</u>

I don't know where to find him, so I walk and my feet head for home, but I can't get beyond the little play park. Ben sticks by me, but he keeps saying "what the hell, Merc?" and I can't make my mouth tell him.

We stop at that crappy little park under the towers and sit on the roundabout like when we were kids.

Ben checks his phone. Nothing. Who would call?

"Maybe we should go wait at the hospital," he says at last.

But I can't. What will I say to Bettina? How will I tell her I let him go?

I just sit on the roundabout. Ben finds a fag somewhere and we share it. The smoke burns down my throat and into my chest and reminds me that I am alive.

"Maybe go home and let your mum clean you up?" Ventures Ben.

Idiot.

I start laughing then. Ben doesn't understand. He looks at me and shakes his head.

"You're a weird one, Merc."

He's not wrong, so I laugh more and then I'm crying and laughing too. Ben tries patting my shoulder, but I tell him to fuck off.

"Okay, then," he says, getting up and looking down at me. "Okay, Merc. I'll go. Reckon I'll go to the hospital and see if there's news."

"It's going to be okay," he says. I know he means it. He just doesn't understand. I say nothing.

"I'll let you know," he says over his shoulder. The kiddie-gate clangs behind him and he is almost gone before I find my voice.

"Ben!" I call. My voice is cracked, like it's forgotten how to work.

I see him stop and he looks back.

"You're a good bloke, Ben," I say.

He knows what I mean and he nods: "you too, Merc."

Then he goes. Tall and steady, ready to save the world. Ben. I'm grateful he is my friend. Romeo's friend.

I am alone in the park, the lights in the towers around me going out as the night deepens.

I have nothing to do but wait.

<u>Dion</u>

It's like a blur and slow motion all at once, me and Ronan half-dragging Kev away down the streets. Tim and his gang are gone, disappearing into the dark like the bad spirits they are and for a while it feels like it's just me and Ronan, with Kev groaning between us.

The sirens sound somewhere behind us, but we are well-clear.

Kev groans. "Hospital," he manages.

There is blood on his shirt and his jeans, but I can't see how much. Me and Ronan head for

A & E across the car park. We're nearly there when Ronan stops.

"Police, mate…" He says.

I don't care. This is Kev we're talking about. Besides, we did nothing wrong. Did we?

"Bullshit," I say and start to move, but Kev pulls his arm away from me.

His face is very pale and his eyes are having trouble focusing, but he looks hard at me and shakes his head.

"I can make it," his voice is scratchy, like it is running out.

"Bullshit," I say again, but Kev pushes me off and starts away across the car park, headed for the white lights of A & E and the line of yellow ambulances.

"Kev!" but he keeps going and Ronan has his hand on my shoulder.

"He'll be okay," he says, "he's tough – he's been here before."

When? Why didn't I know? Suddenly I feel like a little kid again, like I know nothing and the world is just too big to cope with. I want to hit Ronan. I want to kill Tim Ashby. But I can't do anything but stand here and wait.

We watch as Kev makes it to the edge of the ambulances, then he just sort-of topples over, like the rope that was pulling him, has run out. I start towards him, but Ronan grabs my arm. While we watch, a paramedic appears, bends and rolls Kev over. It isn't long before a gurney is wheeled out and Kev disappears through the automatic doors of the hospital.

Blank.

That's all there is.

We stand there in the car park looking at the white lights of the A & E door. Somewhere an engine starts up.

It seems like an age before my brain starts to work. Ronan looks at me. He isn't much of a talker at the best of times. I wonder how old he is. He looks old.

Nothing to say. We just walk away. There's nothing else to do.

When Ronan stops and puts his fist out awkwardly, I know that, somehow, all the madness that has happened has just stopped. Like the end of a Soap episode: `tune in tomorrow for the next thrilling episode.'

 Ronan doesn't look me in the eye: "better get home now…" It's like he is talking to a kid or something, heading home after hanging out on a corner.

I bump his fist and nod and he walks away, alone.

It's a weird feeling: I know it's just me here on the deserted street with the sounds of the late-night city coming at me in far-off beeps and the occasional siren; but I am not here. As if I am caught in some alternate universe where reality isn't reality. The ghost of Kev hangs on my shoulder and I can feel the weight of him.

I don't want to go home. I don't want to deal with Dad's questions.

I try to think about what will be happening to Kev. Will he need blood? Stitches? But an image of white hair coming out of the dark like a banner keeps interrupting.

It was his mate, I suddenly realise, the bloke who came out of the dark to pull Tim Ashby off of Kev. It was his mate who was down, with the girl screaming. That was why he came running out of the dark like a ghost, white hair blazing. He saw his mate down on the ground – and then he saw me. I saw the ice eyes; felt him.

What if he thinks it was me?

It's not about the police and blame. It's just… what if he thinks it was me?

My feet move without any commands. I don't know where I am headed, but my feet are walking a path they seem to know, so I just walk.

<u>Mercutio</u>

I dunno what he's doing here – it's not where he lives. But here he is, walking up to the kiddie gate like he knows it. He stands, his hand on the gate, looking up at the towers as if he's trying to figure something out. He doesn't see me. Just stands there, like he's waiting.

I watch him.

Dion.

I think of all the times he was a bastard at school. Think of the shed. Think of his face turning away in an alley. There's a feel of sick in my throat.

"Dion."

He doesn't jump, but his eyes are wide as he scans the play park for me. His knuckles catch the light as his hand tightens on the gate.

"It wasn't me." He says.

I say nothing. He was there. He knows it. I know it.

"It wasn't me," he repeats. His body is tensed, shoulders stiff and elbows bent. Coiled. But he pushes open the gate and it squeaks and clangs as he comes in. He's still not sure where I am, so I stand up.

He breathes out then – a long slow sigh. "Sorry about your mate…"

I don't know what happens in my head. Before I know what I am doing, I am hitting him in the face, my knuckles connecting with bone and cartilage. Hot rage feels like it will burn up my heart and all I can see is Romeo down in the alleyway that smells of piss and Dion running away.

He just takes it.

I hit him and hit him and hit him. I'm hitting him so hard that I have to hold him up and his face splits into slashes and his lips burst open. But he just takes it.

And then, just like that, the fire is out and I let him go.

He just slips down against the gate, like a rag.

"It wasn't me…" he mumbles through his broken mouth.

I am shaking so badly that I can't stand up, so I sit down next to him, my back against the bars of the fence. I don't even know that I am crying until he reaches up and touches my face with the back of his hand.

"It wasn't me." He says again. I don't want to believe him, but I do.

It makes no difference any-way.

His hand is still on my face and I can feel him looking at me. I want to shrug him off, but I want him to stay too, to have someone touch me.

"S'okay," he says. And then he is holding my hand. Square, strong fingers wrap around my palm. Holding my hand, stopping the shakes.

We just sit. There is nothing to say.

I think of Romeo somewhere under white lights, his life pumping out through a hole in his chest.

His voice saying Tannita's name.

Not me. Her. There under the light. Not me.

And Bettina. I picture her in a hospital chair, waiting to hear.

They are a million miles from me now. The emptiness stretches into me like dying.

I sit in the park, the bars cold against my back and hold Dion's hand.

"Mark," he says at last.

When I look at him I see that one of his eyes is swollen shut and his mouth is a mess. But he is looking at me. Seeing me.

It just happens.

I kiss him: feel the give of his lips, taste the metal in his blood, feel how he kisses me back.

I think of Romeo. The way his smile is like sunshine. The laughter in his voice. The blood pumping out of his chest.

I unwrap Dion's fingers from my hand, peeling them away like sticking plaster. I find that I am cold when I stand up, but the shakes have stopped and my head feels cool and clear.

I don't look at him, but I know he is looking at me.

Everything makes sense, as if a huge puzzle has slotted into place and the map is clear. I can still taste his blood in my mouth and I don't wipe it away.

"Mark," he says and I hear that he wants me to stay.

But I ease past him through the kiddie gate and it clangs shut behind me.

"Mark!" he says again.

For a moment I stand and look at him, his face all smashed and his eyes trying to say my name.

"Mark?"

But it's no good.

"Sorry, Dion," and part of me means it. "That's not my name."

I walk away across the billion miles of who I was.

Mercutio. Like Mercury.

The metal that flows like water.

The morning is coming quickly now. Far wispy clouds glow pink against the pale sky.

He knows where her stash is – she's never made a secret of it and he feels nothing as he counts off ten 20's. He reckons she owes him.

There's a 6:20 train out of Kingscross to Edinburgh. He'll need to move if he's going to make it.

There's not a lot to pack: a couple of shirts, a pair of jeans and a transformers sweatshirt that is way too small.

The bloodied clothes are in a heap by the door and long habit urges him to tidy them away, but in the end, he reckons she owes him, so he leaves them there. Strange testimony to what he is leaving behind.

He has tried to finish the letters, but nothing else will come, so he stuffs them in his pocket. He can't find envelopes, so he will slide them under Bettina's door – unfinished, unpacked.

There won't be a note for Aggie.

When he thinks of her, he hears a ragged coughing from across the hall. Already it is the sound of a stranger. Something just as meaningless as the click of the door closing.

He doesn't look back as he pulls the door of the cold little boxroom and walks the short passage where the walls are peeling. There are no keys in his pocket as he eases the door shut.

Bettina's flat is dark and his heart aches for a moment for all that light and warmth and the smell of pancakes.

But what's done is done and he slips the notes under the door, like whispers against the floor.

Then it is just a door and it is easy to turn his back and walk away down the stairs that stay grey, even though the morning is glowing into orange and warm.

Outside the blackbirds are trilling and the first cars have begun their mumblings. A small wind catches at the pale hair. He doesn't stop to look back.

About The Author:

MJ Whyman was once a journalist and then a teacher.
She lives in Shropshire and is happiest with a book and
a cup of tea.

She has previously published three collections of
poetry. This is her first novel.